Sons of a Parisian Dynasty

*Claiming their legacy. Finding their family.
Meeting their match!*

With the retirement of their patriarch, the renowned Causcelle triplets are taking over an aristocratic empire! These gorgeous yet media-shy billionaires are stepping into the spotlight to make their mark on Paris.

Firstborn Nic has taken over the hotel branch of the business—and immediately caused a scandal with the company's new attorney! While Raoul is heading up the rest of the corporation—at least until mysteriously absent Jean-Louis can be found...

But while these brooding siblings are taking the business world by storm, their hearts are completely off-limits—when you're this wealthy, love always comes with a catch, right? Until they meet the women who show them just how wrong they are!

Find out who tames Nic in
Capturing the CEO's Guarded Heart

See the return of Jean-Louis in
Falling for Her Secret Billionaire

And dive into Raoul's story in
Billionaire's Second Chance in Paris

All available now!

Dear Reader,

This trilogy, Sons of a Parisian Dynasty, begins with the mention of a crime in the background of book one that is fully exposed by book three, *Billionaire's Second Chance in Paris*, which puts the hero and heroine in difficulty.

I love an element of uncertainty involved in the romance and hope you love it, too.

Enjoy!

Rebecca Winters

Billionaire's Second Chance in Paris

Rebecca Winters

Recycling programs
for this product may
not exist in your area.

ISBN-13: 978-1-335-73716-8

Billionaire's Second Chance in Paris

Copyright © 2023 by Rebecca Winters

For questions and comments about the quality of this book,
please contact us at CustomerService@Harlequin.com.

Harlequin Enterprises ULC
22 Adelaide St. West, 41st Floor
Toronto, Ontario M5H 4E3, Canada
www.Harlequin.com

Printed in U.S.A.

Rebecca Winters lives in Salt Lake City, Utah. With canyons and high alpine meadows full of wildflowers, she never runs out of places to explore. They, plus her favorite vacation spots in Europe, often end up as backgrounds for her romance novels—because writing is her passion, along with her family and church. Rebecca loves to hear from readers. If you wish to email her, please visit her website at rebeccawinters.net.

Books by Rebecca Winters

Harlequin Romance

Sons of a Parisian Dynasty

Capturing the CEO's Guarded Heart
Falling for Her Secret Billionaire

The Baldasseri Royals

Reclaiming the Prince's Heart
Falling for the Baldasseri Prince
Second Chance with His Princess

Secrets of a Billionaire

The Greek's Secret Heir
Unmasking the Secret Prince

Visit the Author Profile page
at Harlequin.com for more titles.

This book is dedicated to my darling sister Kathie, who loves a dose of danger in some of the romances she reads. She has always championed my writing.

Praise for
Rebecca Winters

"This is the first book that I have read by this author but definitely not the last as it is an amazing story. I definitely recommend this book as it is so well written and definitely worth reading."

—*Goodreads* on *How to Propose to a Princess*

PROLOGUE

FOR ONCE, seventeen-year-old Fleurine Dumotte had the house to herself. Her out-
of-control father would be working at the
Causcelle dairy until late, thank goodness.
Her sweet, wonderful mother had gone to
town in La Racineuse with her two siblings
to shop. She'd be gone a long time. Fleurine
had volunteered to do the laundry for the five-
member household in order to be alone.

Knowing there wasn't a moment to lose,
she did her chores in record time. Then she
got busy making bread, shaping pieces of
it into five-inch boy figures. Normally she
placed raisins down their tummies to look like
buttons. But these were for Raoul Causcelle,
so she baked the figures without adornment.

After they cooled, she put tiny dobs of frosting for buttons and added little *pépites de chocolat*. She'd made his favorite milk bread *mannele*. He loved the chocolate on top. It would be her going-away gift to him, but no one could ever know about it. Not even her mother. Her terrifying father forbade her from being with any boy, so her feelings for Raoul had always remained a secret from everyone.

He'd seen her in town helping with the marketing yesterday and had asked her to meet him at the west hay barn at the end of his work today. They could talk one last time while he did his chores, but her excitement was swallowed up in despair. The day after tomorrow he'd be leaving home with his brothers to go to college in Paris hundreds of miles away.

Fleurine had been born and raised on the Causcelle estate. All the kids in the area had gone to the same schools. She and Raoul were eleven months apart. Over the last two years he'd found dozens of ways to meet her accidentally at school and on her way home after the bell rang.

The knowledge that Raoul was leaving

had become unbearable, and she'd wanted to do something for him. After wrapping the *mannele* in a bag, she cleaned up the kitchen so her father would never know what she'd done. Next, Fleurine hurried into the bedroom she shared with her thirteen-year-old sister, Emma. Their eleven-year-old brother, Marti, had his own room.

Fleurine had no choice but to put on one of her ugly white dresses that fell below the knee. It had long sleeves that looked like a nursing uniform from a hundred years ago. He'd never seen her in anything else. She wished she were allowed to go to mass like her friends and wear something pretty. How she hated her brown shoes that laced up to the ankles. So many wishes had never been fulfilled...

The women in their household weren't allowed to wear makeup or perfume or cut their hair. All she could do was brush hers that hung down her back. She'd been forbidden to use ribbons or barrettes. Modern styles of clothes were out of the question. She could still hear her father say, "Fleur and Emma Dumotte, you'll live in my house like proper daughters of the Jura-Souboz where your ancestors came from and obey my rules!"

His despotic eighteenth-century rules!

Not wanting to feel pain today, she raced out of the house with her gift and climbed on her bike. Raoul had always been a hard worker and obeyed his nice-looking widower father, who everyone knew had high expectations for him and his brothers. The country's renowned billionaire Louis Causcelle kept his children close. Fleurine had seen him on several occasions but had never met him. She was pained by her father's hatred for the patriarch of the Causcelle dynasty and his family, especially his triplet sons.

On her approach, she saw Raoul's bike outside the barn. She rode hers around the back. She didn't dare leave it where her father could see it from the road on his way home from the dairy.

"There you are, Fleurine," she heard Raoul say while she rested her bike against the barn. He'd walked in through the back to find her. "I hoped you'd be able to make it." His smile lit up her universe.

No one knew her as Fleurine. Only Raoul had started calling her that name last year.

He'd said it was because her eyes reminded him of the violet flowers growing in the northern pasture. To her mind, her eyes were a boring gray with tinges of violet. But since he'd given her that name, she'd begun thinking of herself as Fleurine. He'd made it sound beautiful.

"Let's take your bike inside." They walked to the front with it and went in the barn where he shut the big door.

Raoul was fun and exciting. He was also so handsome it made her breath catch. His dancing black eyes and black hair thrilled her as much as his smile. Sometimes he resembled a dashing pirate. She'd always felt insipid around him by comparison.

No young men in school, let alone France, matched the looks of the tall, gorgeous and well-built Causcelle triplet sons. Her girlfriends had told her their pictures had been in all the newspapers and magazines and on TV, but her father didn't allow radio, TV or printed matter in their home.

"I had to do the laundry first, or I would have come sooner. Here." She handed him the bag. "I baked these for you."

His intense gaze made her feel warm all

over. He opened it and pulled out one of her treats. "Let's find out if you're still the best cook in France."

Heat crept into her face. "Don't be ridiculous."

"I swear I'm telling the truth. I've eaten your treats before. You could run your own five-star cooking school." On that note he took a bite and ended up devouring the whole thing with those perfect white teeth. "Yup. You deserve the grand prize for these. Let me thank you properly and give you whatever you want."

Whatever she wanted? Would that Fleurine had the temerity to tell him she wanted the one thing he could never give her. Her father had forbidden her and her siblings to have anything to do with the Causcelle family. If they ever did, they would pay the ultimate price. He terrified them. What an absurd, foolish girl she'd been to have secret dreams about a life with Raoul.

Fleurine had been dreading the moment when he would leave the estate. The end of their childhood had come. To a degree, childhood had been the common denominator that made a more equal playing field for them to be together, but no longer. There wasn't a thing she could do about this parting of their worlds, and already she was dying inside. To face a day without Raoul meant no more adventure or wonder. No more feeling alive.

"Mind if I thank you in the way I've wanted to for a long time?"

Something in his tone sounded different. "What do you mean?"

"Have you ever been kissed by one of the guys around here, Fleurine? Really kissed? I've noticed Remy and Thomas. They never leave you alone."

"They're just friends." Her heart pounded in her throat.

"Do you put me in the same category as *just a friend*?"

She averted her eyes. "A good friend. Are you trying to embarrass me?"

"Anything but. I'd like to know if there's some guy you're interested in on the estate you've kept secret from me."

"How can you ask me that?" Her voice shook. "You know my father."

"Forget your father for a minute. Is there someone you care about and have been alone with?"

She shivered. "That's private, Raoul."

"So there *is* a guy—" He sounded upset.

Her head flew back. "What if I asked you if there's a girl on the estate *you've* kissed?"

He shifted his weight. "Do you want to know the answer? Or aren't you interested enough to find out?"

Fleurine shook her head. "I wouldn't dare ask you. It's none of my business."

"Maybe it's because you're frightened of the answer. Yes, I've kissed a few."

"I think I'd better go."

She turned to leave, but he grasped her arm. "You *are* frightened."

"Please, Raoul. I don't know what you want from me."

He inhaled sharply. "The truth. Nothing more, nothing less. For once in our lives, we're truly alone. I know you're frightened of your father, but he's nowhere around to hear us."

"What truth?" she cried, not understanding him. Something was wrong.

"That you love me as much as I love you!" The interior of the barn resounded with his declaration. "Isn't love the reason you came at the risk of your father finding out? Isn't love why you brought me this gift?"

A gasp escaped her lips. She backed away from him. "E-even if the answer were yes," she said, "you couldn't possibly love me, Raoul Causcelle. Not *you,* who could have any girl, I mean *any* girl, in the world. Are you telling the Dumotte daughter, who's been told to go back to the dark ages where our family belongs, that you love *me*?"

"Don't talk about yourself that way, Fleurine."

"You haven't lived in my skin, Raoul. I'm the offspring of old man Dumotte who lights fires and would have been the first to set a torch to Jeanne d'Arc. Did you know *he* and the demented friends in their cult were the ones who set fire to the monastery when he was a young teenager?

"He helped murder all those monks to get rid of your father's brother-in-law Gregoire. My father was taught to hate every Catholic before his family moved here from Switzerland and started working for your family. He's forbidden our family from ever stepping inside a Catholic church."

"I've suspected it for a long time."

"He's insane, but most of all he hates your father for marrying your mother."

Raoul moved closer. His black eyes flashed. "What do you mean?"

"He wanted Delphine Ronfleur for himself, but she wanted your father and married him. My mother broke down one day and told me everything. She lives in fear of him. So do I. If she tries to leave or expose him, he has threatened to kill the whole family. Lately he's been watching me."

"I knew that was the reason why you've tried to be so careful around me," Raoul murmured.

"Then, you should know there's never been anyone else for me but you, and there never will be. But you're the son of the man my father despises. I'm afraid *you're* another object of his hatred now. Run to Paris while there's still time and stay safe! He mustn't ever see us alone together. I'm a nothing who's not worthy of you, Raoul."

"Don't you ever say things like that, Fleurine." He reached out and crushed her in his arms, holding her until her thrashing stopped, but her body kept heaving sobs. "I've always loved you and have sensed deep down you felt the same way. Let me kiss you so I can show you how I feel. We'll deal with everything else later."

Fleurine couldn't believe this was happening. Raoul honestly loved *her*?

"Right now, we need this time together before I have to leave. Once I'm gone, we know letters and phone calls will be impossible." He lowered his head. First, he planted soft kisses near her mouth then her lips. She kissed him back the same way. Slowly they melded.

Their kisses grew deeper and longer. She threw her arms around his neck and clung to him, exhilarated by new sensations of being kissed and held in his arms. If only this could go on forever.

"I love you, Fleurine. I can't remember a time when I didn't."

"I won't be able to live without you!" she cried, kissing him over and over again.

"All these years we've shared everything but this. I have plans for us. When I come home at Christmas, you'll have turned eighteen the day before. I'll make all the arrangements, and we'll run away immediately to get married at the church in Paris. Your father won't know what happened until it's too late."

"Oh, Raoul. *Your* father would never permit it."

He kissed every feature. "Don't worry. He married my mother in their teens and won't be able to raise an argument. We'll live in Paris in an apartment. You're the smartest girl at school and can start college. We'll go together, and I'll pay for it, and after graduation we'll buy our own home while I work for the family business. We'll be away from your father and live the rest of our lives the way I've always dreamed."

"If I thought that could happen…" She returned his kisses with shocking hunger.

Suddenly the barn door lifted. In the late-afternoon light she saw her father, a tall, powerfully built man with a ruddy complexion and beard. He held a hunting rifle aimed at Raoul.

"Get your hands off my daughter or I'll shoot you dead this instant."

Fleurine pulled out of Raoul's arms. How had her father known she was here? "We weren't doing anything wrong!" she cried in absolute horror. "I was just saying goodbye to him."

She heard him cock the rifle. "Get in the truck, Fleur."

"Don't hurt him!" she screamed.

"Do as I say. If I ever catch the two of you together again, you'll both be dead. You've shamed me, daughter."

Knowing what he was capable of, she ran out of the barn to the truck. Before she got in, she threw up, terrified of what he'd do to Raoul. As she heaved her trembling body into the truck, her father got in on the other side. He put the rifle on the rack behind their heads.

When she looked back, she saw Raoul standing at the barn entrance.

Dieu merci he was still alive!

CHAPTER ONE

Paris, France,
late August, ten years later.

RAOUL CAUSCELLE ENTERED Causcelle head-quarters. He climbed the marble staircase of the converted palace to the second floor and knocked on the private office door of the CEO.

The new head of the Causcelle empire looked up. "Raoul—"

"*Eh bien*, Pascal."

"I'm glad you got my message. Thanks for coming. Since I knew you were already in town on business, this is perfect timing. I need your input."

"I like dropping by my old stomping grounds. It gives me an excuse to see you." Raoul walked into the office. They hugged before he sat down on a chair near the desk. "How's Janelle and the family?"

"We couldn't be better."

"And Oncle Blaise?"

"Papa is still in heaven teaching at the university and writing more books. Tell me about my Oncle Louis."

"It's a miracle Papa is still hanging in there with his bad heart."

"That's amazing. Hey, I hear Jean-Louis was discharged from the military and came home to get married privately."

Raoul nodded. "Something like that. Now that he and Nic have wives, they walk around like grinning bears. Papa has rallied a little since Jean-Louis's return."

Pascal smiled. "I'm glad to hear it."

"Just so you know, Papa asked me to tell you you're doing a superb job of running the corporation. That's my opinion too. He couldn't be happier with you."

"I appreciate that, but it's early days yet. Taking over for you and Nic has been an enormous challenge. I couldn't do it without my co-CEO, George."

"I agree his legal help is invaluable. Papa always said George was his right-hand man.

Please tell me you want to stay on as CEO."
Raoul had always liked his cousin. Outside of
his brothers, Pascal was the only other man
he'd ever confided in.

"You guessed it a long time ago. I *love* what
I do."

"It shows, and that's all I needed to hear.
Now, tell me what it is you need."

"First, I want to hear how *you* are doing.
You know what I mean. What's going on with
you and Mademoiselle Mornay? I hear she's
crazy about you."

He eyed Pascal. "The truth?"

"Uh-oh."

"I wish I felt the same way about her."

Last night Lisette Mornay had begged
Raoul not to leave Paris yet. The new marketing consultant for Causcelle's *parfume-
rie* wasn't satisfied with an occasional dinner
with him when he came to Paris on estate
business. She wanted more. Raoul found her
interesting, but he wasn't emotionally involved. It was why he didn't let her know
he'd decided to stay in Paris one more day
to help Pascal.

Raoul had dated many women for years,
but he never felt compelled to take the rela-

tionship to its ultimate level. He ached for marriage like his brothers. But no matter how many women he spent time with, the desire that would lead to marriage and commitment had never happened.

"After all these years, it's the same old problem, right?"

"I'm stuck, cousin." Raoul hadn't told anyone Dumotte had threatened him and Fleurine ten years ago, but Pascal and his brothers knew he'd loved her from an early age. They encouraged him to keep looking until the right woman came along.

"She's out there somewhere, Raoul. You're still young with a whole world of love ahead of you yet."

He'd thought he had a whole world of love ahead of him at eighteen when he'd been desperately in love. But it had ended in disaster. The only love of Raoul's life—the sweetest, most angelic girl on earth who neither asked nor expected anything from him—had been snatched away at gunpoint. He never saw her again, and he'd been forced to leave for Paris the next day with his brothers.

A month later word reached him about Fleurine from his oncle Raimond, who ran the estate at La Racineuse. He learned she'd moved to Switzerland and had married the son of her father's Swiss friend. The news had gutted Raoul.

For the last ten years he'd been with dozens of women like Lisette, but they were worldly and more material-minded, the antithesis of the woman he'd loved. Fleurine had possessed an untouched quality he'd never found in another woman. As such, his love life hadn't made sense since that horrific moment in the hay barn years ago.

"I appreciate what you're saying, Pascal. I want to believe it… But enough about me for the moment."

"No, no. Don't change the subject. Janelle and I are not giving up on you. In fact, my wife has met a woman she believes would be a perfect match for you. So I'm inviting you for dinner tonight. She'll be there, and we won't take no for an answer."

He eyed Pascal. "You're a good man." He couldn't turn him down. "I'll be glad to come. Now, tell me what's going on."

Pascal sat forward. "George and I are planning to acquire Rayonner-Tech in the Eighth Arrondissement for the Causcelle Corporation. But the recent death of the principal software engineer has left a vacancy. Since then, Rayonner-Tech has received a flood of qualified applicants.

"The person with the most outstanding reviews so far is an engineer still working at Aire-Tech under their CEO, Philippe Charbon. She's been there five years since receiving her master's degree at Paris-Saclay University. Her name is Laure Millet.

"Despite her excellent credentials, George and I feel she should have at least ten years' experience to be the *chief* software engineer. We thought if you sat in on the interview with the CEO, Jules Vaugier, at Rayonner-Tech, you'd get a feel if she could handle the position. You'll be our eyes and ears for this last interview. We can't buy the company until we have more information about the engineer who will fill this position. I value your intuition on this sort of thing."

"I'll be happy to do it."

"*Merveilleux!* The interview with the CEO will be held in their conference room at three o'clock on the main floor. After you've sat in and listened, give me a verdict at dinner." Pascal squinted at him. "Who knows? Maybe our guest will capture the attention of the only single Causcelle billionaire triplet left on the planet."

"*Tu dis n'importe quoi*," Raoul muttered.

"I'm *not* full of it, cousin. The press can't get enough of you. Nor can the women apparently. Every month in the news there's another photo of you with your latest gorgeous date. But Janelle swears you'll really like *this* one. All I'm allowed to say is that she's different. Only your Causcelle genes will let you know if we've helped you solve your quest for a lifetime companion. Her looks you'll have to determine for yourself."

His comment forced a laugh out of Raoul who'd heard enough. "You've actually managed to intrigue me. I'm going back to the *palais*. After I sit in on that interview, I'll see you at dinner. Thanks."

Pascal's eyes twinkled. "I have a feeling this evening might prove to change your life. See you later."

Raoul got to his feet. Though he had little hope of developing a meaningful relationship with a woman at this point, his mood had been lightened by being with Pascal. He left headquarters and headed on foot for the

Causcelle family hotel a block away called the *palais,* another palace. He and his brothers had lived there while they'd gone to university.

It had now been converted into a hostel for military vets who could live there free while getting trained for jobs. Jean-Louis had turned it into his dream project. Two of the twelve suites were still reserved for family.

Both his brothers had moved on and found the kind of fulfilling happiness with their wives that had eluded Raoul. He was ecstatic for them. But deep down he envied them in every particle of his being.

While Fleurine Dumotte was working in her office at Aire-Tech, she checked her watch. A second job interview had been arranged for her at Rayonner-Tech at three. In an hour she'd be meeting again with the CEO, Jules Vaugier.

She'd been so happy at Aire-Tech until her boss had hired a new software engineer named Paul Loti. He was smart and attractive, and from day one he'd let her know he wanted to date her. She had gone out to dinner with him once, but the magic hadn't been there, and she'd turned him down for another date. From then on things grew difficult because he didn't understand why she wouldn't go out with him again.

It alarmed her that he refused to leave her alone. When she told him she only wanted to be work friends, he insisted he'd fallen in love with her. If she'd only give him a chance. Paul had asked her if she was hung up on someone else. She'd told him there wasn't anyone. He didn't like it that she'd turned him down.

Fleurine came to the point that she couldn't bear to work with Paul every day knowing how he felt. He always waited for her before and after hours to talk. She couldn't concentrate on her job any longer but didn't want to get him in trouble by telling her boss.

In truth, the only man she'd ever loved had been driven off by her father ten years earlier with a death threat. After the ghastly confrontation in the estate barn, Fleurine never saw Raoul Causcelle again. That very night her father took her to his sister's home in Switzerland where the older woman kept a close watch on her. Four months later Fleurine turned eighteen and ran away before she was forced to marry the son of her father's friend.

Since that time, she'd studied and worked her heart out to become a success. She'd dated quite a few guys, but nothing serious had developed. After talking it over with her friend, Deline, she realized the only thing to do about Paul was resign and work for another company.

She'd seen several openings online at different software companies. The one at Rayonner-Tech for the position of principal software engineer drew her attention. They were renowned for being the best. It was an ambitious move on her part to apply for the position since she'd never been a chief software engineer and didn't have the years of experience required. Yet, because of her excellent work record, they'd allowed her to interview. This second interview gave her hope they were willing to give her a chance.

Rayonner-Tech had a reputation for being outstanding, and they paid an awesome salary. If they still decided they wanted a person with more experience, then she'd interview for a position somewhere else, even if it meant finding work in another city.

She left her office at two thirty and drove there. At five to three she entered the main building where the woman at the front desk she'd met before named Gabrielle greeted her.

"Mademoiselle Millet, you're right on time. Monsieur Vaugier will be down in a minute. Follow me to the conference room." She got up from her desk. "The other gentleman has already arrived."

Fleurine had legally changed her name to Laure Millet ten years ago. She'd done it to prevent her father from tracking her. She also knew that with the Causcelle headquarters based in Paris where Raoul would be in and out, she didn't dare use her birth name. "I didn't know this interview would include anyone else."

Gabrielle turned to her as they walked. "It's Raoul Causcelle, representing the Causcelle Corporation. They are considering buying Rayonner-Tech. Monsieur Vaugier asked him to sit in on this interview."

Raoul? Fleurine's Raoul?

He was in the conference room?

Just hearing his name came as such a shock, she tripped and fell.

"Oh, no!" the woman cried. "Are you all right?" She lent a hand to help her get up.

Fleurine couldn't think. "Forgive me, Gabrielle. I'm afraid I wasn't watching where I was going in these new high heels. I've hurt my bad knee," she lied, needing an excuse to get away quickly. "Please tell Monsieur Vaugier how sorry I am, but I can't be interviewed right now. I'll call him later. If you could just help me to the entrance, I'll drive to the hospital and have it looked at."

"Of course. Lean on me. I'm so sorry this happened, *mademoiselle*."

"So am I." Fleurine faked a limp as the woman walked her all the way out to her car in the side parking lot. "This is so kind of you."

"Don't give it another thought."

"I can't thank you enough."

Once the receptionist was out of sight, Fleurine started the engine and drove back to her office. The knowledge that Raoul had been inside that conference room had frightened her to the core of her being.

He didn't know it, but after that horrific moment at the hay barn ten years ago—once her father had her under lock and key at his sister's house—he'd hired a man in the cult to watch Raoul wherever he went 24-7. Garber had vowed to kill Raoul if he ever caught him with Fleurine again.

Her mother had written all that information in a letter she'd hidden for Fleurine to find before she was kidnapped by her father to Switzerland. Her mother had told her everything and begged her to believe that her father would never stop if it took a lifetime. He'd been a madman since his teens and was living for the day he caught her and Raoul together so he could kill both of them.

Fleurine had lived with that dire warning for ten years and broke out in a cold sweat. Even after all this time, the man or men he'd hired could be outside Rayonner-Tech *right now*, watching and waiting for Raoul to be caught with her. After years of protecting Raoul from her father by staying away from him, how could this have happened?

Surely Raoul didn't know the true identity of Laure Millet. How could he, when Fleurine had disappeared from his life a decade ago after changing her name and appearance? Nothing made sense.

Once back in her private office, she phoned Monsieur Vaugier's office, and a secretary answered. Fleurine apologized for what had happened outside the conference room. She explained about hurting her knee and that it would require surgery. She thanked him for the chance to interview with him. Maybe another time.

On that note, she hung up and sat there with her head in her hands. She couldn't stop trembling. Had Raoul somehow discovered who Laure Millet really was? How was that even possible? In all these years there'd never been a slip.

A knock sounded on the door. "Laure?"

She jumped. Paul's voice. Of course. He just wouldn't leave her alone. "Yes?"

"I saw you come in. Do you have a minute?"

"Not right now. I'm sorry."

"It's almost closing time. I was hoping you'd let me to take you to dinner so we could really talk."

"Paul, we *have* talked, and you know I just want to be friends. Please don't ask me again."

"So you haven't changed your mind?"

"No, I'm sorry."

Go away. Please, go away. I'm dying inside.

There was something seriously wrong with him.

For the next little while she tried to get into a project she'd been working on, but her fears made it impossible to concentrate. After giving up, she reached for the phone to call Deline, an accountant at Samaritaine.

Fleurine had met her a year ago while solving a software problem at the department store. They were single and close in age. Before long they became good friends and attended mass together. It felt so good after being forbidden to go to church. Hopefully Deline could come over to Fleurine's apartment this evening. They would order Chinese and talk.

She'd just started to tap the digits on her phone when there was another knock on the door. "Laure?"

It was Paul again. Now she really was angry. "What is it?"

"As I was leaving, a tall, powerful-looking man came in. I told him it was after hours and he'd have to come again on Monday. He told me he had an appointment with you, but he found out you'd had an accident. He wanted to know if you were in the building.

"His aggressive attitude concerned me, and I realized you don't tell someone like him anything. After asking him to wait, I came back up here to warn you about him. If I don't go downstairs in a minute, he'll come up any-way."

Alarmed, she hung up and got to her feet. A tall, powerful, *aggressive* man? Was it pos-sible her father had found her after all these years? How did he know she'd fallen? Had he been tracking Raoul? How had a connec-tion been made?

"Did you ask his name?"

"No. I doubt he would have given it to me."

"Did he have a beard?"

"No."

Maybe he'd finally found her and had come to Paris himself. All he had to do was follow her to that interview where Raoul was wait-ing. No doubt he'd shaved in order to trick her. Fleurine gasped at the thought and felt sick to her stomach. If there was going to be another murder like the ones he and his friends had committed in their teens, then the police would know about it this time.

"Just a minute." She grabbed the phone and called 1-1-2. After reporting a life-threatening emergency at this address, she hung up. "Come inside quick and close the door, Paul!"

After he'd done her bidding, he stared at

her. "You're as white as a sheet, Laure. What's going on?"

"I don't know. But if this is what I think it is, I need you for a witness. I've called the police. Don't go downstairs. Stay here and flatten yourself against the wall behind the door. When he comes up and bursts in, I don't want you getting hurt." She would be her father's first target.

"You really mean it, don't you?"

Yes. Her father had his own arsenal of weapons on the estate and was an expert marksman. For all she knew, he'd already shot Raoul at Rayonner-Tech before coming for her.

Paul moved over to the wall. She stayed at her desk and prayed the police would get here in time.

CHAPTER TWO

RAOUL GOT TO his feet as Jules Vaugier entered the conference room at Rayonner-Tech. "Thanks so much for coming to this second interview, Monsieur Causcelle. I believe this engineer could be the right one even if she doesn't have as much experience. Since your corporation is considering buying Rayonner-Tech, I thought it appropriate that you sit in on this meeting."

"Our CEO asked if I would do this since I'm in Paris. I'm happy to follow through." Raoul knew Pascal was anxious to get this situation resolved before any negotiation took place.

They'd just started to talk when the receptionist came into the conference room looking anxious. "I'm afraid Mademoiselle Millet tripped and fell on her way in here and has driven herself to the hospital to see about her injured knee. She said she'd call you later, Monsieur Vaugier."

"I'm surprised she could drive," Raoul said to Jules. "Since I'm free, I'll check the nearest hospitals and InstaCare facilities to learn how she is. Then I'll get back to you."

"Thank you, Raoul. I truly appreciate that."

He left the building, knowing this was urgent. Pascal would want to hear what happened right away. After a half hour of inquiries, he discovered that a Laure Millet hadn't reported into any hospitals or care facilities in the area.

Curious about that, Raoul decided to drive to her office. Perhaps someone at Aire-Tech knew what was going on or could give Raoul her phone number. Pascal was depending on him.

"It's closing time," he was told by a thirty-ish man when he walked into Aire-Tech. The man's hostile attitude surprised him.

"I'm here to find out if Mademoiselle Millet is in the building. She missed an appointment because of a fall. I'd like to know if she's all right. If you can't help me, I'll go up to her office." The building directory indicated Laure Millet had an office on the second floor.

The man shook his head. He seemed to have taken an odd dislike to Raoul. "Hold on. I'm one of the engineers here. I'll go up and find out," he muttered before taking the elevator.

Raoul waited a few minutes. When the man didn't materialize, he was convinced something was off. Deciding not to wait any longer, he had started for the elevator when a contingent of armed police burst in the entrance of the building. In a second, he was surrounded. The lead officer and two others went up in the elevator. The other two remained with Raoul.

One of them turned to him. "Who are you, and why are you here? It's after hours."

"I'm Raoul Causcelle from the Causcelle Corporation. I came to see one of the engineers. She had a fall before she could make it to a private job interview at Rayonner-Tech scheduled at three. I came here to find out if she was here and if she was all right.

"One of the engineers was just leaving the building. I told him I wanted to talk to Laure Millet if she were here. He went back up to see if he could find her, but he never came down. Frankly I'm glad you're here to investigate."

The officer nodded. "You'll have to stay here for now." He radioed someone while the night security guard came down a hall and locked the front door.

A few minutes later the other officers reappeared. The lead officer flashed Raoul a glance. "The situation has been resolved. You're free to go up, Monsieur Causcelle."

On that brief note the police left the building. Raoul passed the engineer coming out of the elevator. He looked upset. After sending Raoul an angry glare, he walked outside past the security guard.

Now it was Raoul's turn to do his own investigating. He went upstairs and headed down the hall to her office. The door had been left open, and he saw a woman seated at a desk in front of a computer. She had attractive dark blond hair highlighted by gold strands. The neck-length cut looked professionally tousled with loose waves that fell from a side part.

Raoul knocked to let her know he was standing there. When she raised her head, the motion exposed her face and throat to his gaze. He hadn't known what to expect. For a moment the world stilled. There was no question he was staring at the most beautiful woman he'd ever laid eyes on in his life.

He walked in, aware of a sweet flowery fragrance coming from her. The open-collared white blouse worn beneath a stunning navy jacket framed her gorgeous oval face and high cheekbones. He noticed her creamy complexion and the pink lipstick on the enticing curvature of her lips.

Incredibly, their shape reminded him of someone else's lips and mouth. Someone from long ago who'd been a young beauty at seventeen… With his pulse hammering in his throat, he moved closer.

A pair of soft gray eyes between dark lashes stared back at him in what he could only describe as wonderment. The subtle lavender eye shadow brought out their violet flecks, taking him back ten years. A moan escaped. It couldn't be, but it was…

"Fleurine—"

"I—I can't believe it's you." Her voice faltered. She'd turned into a raving beauty.

He could hardly breathe. "You're so lovely,

I can't believe my own eyes. After all these years... To think it was you, not Laure Millet, coming in for that interview. You've changed your name."

"Yes." In the twinkling of an eye, she'd paled. "A great deal has changed since the last time we saw each other, Raoul. What terrifies me is that even if you know that's not my birth name, you should *never* have come up here."

Her comment puzzled him. He moved closer. "The receptionist at Rayonner-Tech said you fell before you could keep your interview. The secretary you phoned explained that you'd need surgery on your knee. But it appears you didn't go to a hospital. I came here to inquire about you for Jules Vaugier. I didn't have a clue I'd find *you* sitting here."

"Thank heaven for that." She gripped the edge of her desk. "Please don't stay here any longer. You need to leave this instant! Run, Raoul!" She'd lost more color.

"Wait a minute." He rubbed the back of his neck trying to take this all in. "What's going on?"

"*My father!* He's after you and always has been. A little while ago Paul told me a man had come here to see me. I asked him to tell the man to call or come on Monday, but he explained this person didn't care it was closing time and seemed aggressive. That intimidated Paul who said you didn't tell a man like him anything."

"The man seemed to take an instant dislike to me."

"Paul can be difficult. I asked him if the man had a beard. He said no, but I could tell he didn't trust him. I started to get nervous and suddenly could imagine my father bursting into my office the way he'd done at the barn. He could have shaved off his beard. I almost died believing he'd finally found me. I asked Paul to stay with me, and I called the police, hoping they could prevent a murder from happening."

Raoul's blood froze in his veins. He leaned on her desk with his fists. "You're not making sense." None of it made sense. Not anything she'd told him or her new name. "What do you mean you thought he'd finally found you?"

She wiped the moisture from her cheeks. "I ran away from my father ten years ago, but that's a long story. The only thing you need to know is that before my father drove me to his sister's in Switzerland that ghastly night, my mother hid a letter with money and my birth certificate inside the lining of my winter coat. She told me he'd hired men to watch your every move whether on or off the estate. She said that no matter how many years it took— even a lifetime—he would never stop until he caught us together and killed both of us."

"He *what*?"

"Four months later, I escaped from my aunt's house. It was Christmas, and my mother had sent me another note in a gift. She said that over the years your father had paid mine an incredible salary for his work running the dairy. That's how he was able to hire certain henchmen to spy on you around the clock over all these years."

"I don't believe it." Raoul was incredulous.

"My mother would never have lied about this. Don't underestimate her on this. He's been playing a waiting game all this time, expecting me to make contact with you at some point. Now that I know it's *you* Paul spoke to downstairs, you'll never know my relief. As for the police, I told them I thought I was in danger from an older man in my past."

"I'm beginning to think you're in danger from this Paul."

"Of course not. The officer said the only man in the building was a man named Raoul Causcelle from the Causcelle Corporation to see me because he learned about the fall before the interview.

"When I heard that, I told the officer I'd made a terrible mistake. The man I feared was in his sixties and probably gray with a beard. After I apologized for the emergency call, they left. I'm so sorry you were caught up in any of this."

"Sorry?" Raoul was ready to explode over a situation that made no sense to him. He was so thrilled to have found her again he couldn't think about anything else.

"Yes! I'm now convinced my father hasn't found me yet, but *your* life is in constant jeopardy. You know what he's capable of. Never doubt it. That's the reason you need to leave the building right now. Go out the same way you came in, and never come near again so his spies don't suspect anything."

The terror in her eyes and voice was so real he had to believe her for now. She'd called the police out of fear. What more proof did he need? He pulled out his cell. "Tell me your phone number, quickly."

"No." She shook her head and put her hands out. "Let this be the end of it. We never met. You understand?"

"But we have!" he declared. "If you don't give it to me, I'm not going anywhere."

"Please, Raoul." Those exquisite violet eyes begged him. "You're still alive."

"And I plan to stay that way. I have sources who can get your cell-phone number, but I would rather you told me."

After a shaken sigh, she said, "All right," and gave it to him. "Now go!"

He sent her a text so she would have his number then put his phone back in his pocket. "If you decide not to answer when I call, those same sources will know your address."

"Enough threats, Raoul. Just leave for your own sake! My father will never have let go of his vendetta. He lives for the excuse to kill you if he finds us together."

Her concern for him tore him up inside. "How soon are you leaving?"

"In a minute, but I go out the rear entrance to my car."

"Is there a security guard?"

"Yes. I'll be fine."

A lot of good that would do if that madman Dumotte had hired thugs who would kidnap her on sight or, worse, because Raoul had been here. "Expect a call from me tonight."

Before he changed his mind, he rushed out of her office and down the hall, taking the stairs instead of the elevator. The night guard opened the front door for him. He hurried around the parking area to his car, keeping an eye open for those who might be following him. En route, he phoned the *palais* and was answered in record time.

"I'm glad it's you, Guy." The man was now running the vet hostel for Jean-Louis.

"*Salut*, Raoul! *Ça va?*"

"I'm not sure, but I believe someone is following me. I'm headed to the *palais* in the silver Lexus right now and should be there in five minutes."

"What can I do for you?"

"Will you talk to the security guys in front and around the side? As I drive in, ask them to check if I'm being followed or if there's someone parked there who could be watching for me. Tell them to get a picture and a license plate if they notice anything suspicious.

I'll check the surveillance-camera footage to-night to see if they've picked up something."

Guy whistled. "Will do."

Raoul hung up, trying to comprehend that at the very lowest ebb of his life, a miracle had just happened. Like a glorious vision, Fleurine had suddenly appeared before him all grown-up. Yet she was still so sweet and breathtaking, it caused him soul-wrenching pain to think of these lost years.

She looked early twenties, not twenty-eight. The transformation from timid school-girl in the eighteenth-century white dress to the stylish female engineer at Aire-Tech blew his mind. For being a married woman with possible children, Fleurine looked untouched. He hadn't seen a wedding ring. When had she and her husband moved from Switzerland to Paris? No gossip on the estate had reached him about that. Again, nothing added up.

He needed to phone Jules and let him know Mademoiselle Millet's knee would heal, but she wouldn't be going in for the interview now. With that call made, he phoned Pascal and told him that something of a personal nature had come up. He was sorry, but he wouldn't be able to make dinner after all.

Raoul explained that the interview had never taken place and the reason. He sent his regrets to Janelle. They'd do this another time.

Once off the phone, Raoul's hands tightened on the steering wheel. He needed answers by tonight or he would go mad.

Ten minutes after Raoul left her office, Fleurine stole out of the building the back way to her green Peugeot. For once Paul didn't appear to be around, thank goodness. After seeing Raoul again, she shook so hard driving home she couldn't believe she'd made it into the garage without having an accident. Thank heaven for this secluded place.

Five years ago, a wealthy older couple living in a large home in the Sixth Arrondissement had advertised for a renter. Fleurine had just received her master's degree in computer science engineering. To her joy she'd been hired at Aire-Tech with a wonderful salary. All she'd needed was a respectable place to live.

A realtor she'd consulted knew of a possibility for her. She could live in a room in this couple's home or take the furnished two-bedroom apartment over their garage with its interior stairway. Fleurine chose the second option. She could be separate yet connected to the owners and feel safe from her father. So far so good, but she was terrified for Raoul.

He'd be calling her before she went to bed. There was no way of stopping him. Paul had been more than right. The fierce fire in Raoul's black eyes she'd looked into a little while ago would silence anyone. Combined with his tall, powerful physique dressed in the kind of expensive dark blue suit that proclaimed him one of *the* Causelle sons, any man would be intimidated.

The handsome eighteen-year-old on the estate with the dashing pirate smile had grown into a breathtaking, just-turned twenty-nine-year-old man. Raoul had always had the most gorgeous wavy black hair imaginable. Along with his brothers, he blew all other men out of the water. There were no words to describe his charisma or masculine beauty.

Fleurine got out of her car and raced up the stairs to the apartment. She'd missed lunch. Maybe if she ate something, she'd stop shaking. After changing into a robe, she hurried into the kitchen barefooted. Soon she'd made coffee and toast. She'd only started to sip the hot liquid at the kitchen table when her phone rang.

One glance at the caller ID confirmed it was Raoul. She had to answer, but the experience of seeing him today had turned her inside out. To think how many thousands of times in the past she would have done anything just to hear his voice again.

She reached for her cell with an unsteady hand and clicked Accept. "Hello?"

"Fleurine?"

"Yes." It was still unbelievable to hear him on the other end.

"Thank you for answering," came Raoul's deep voice. "Where are you?"

Her heart was in her throat. "I'm home."

"Does your husband know what happened a little while ago?"

Fleurine almost dropped the phone. "What did you say?"

"You don't have to pretend with me. Everyone on the estate knows you got married ten years ago and have been living in Switzerland. What I don't understand is why I never heard any talk that you were in Paris now."

A groan of disbelief escaped her lips. "Raoul, I didn't get married. I'm still *single*!

My mother told me my father invented that lie. He spread that story at the dairy in order to explain my absence from the estate."

"What?"

She gripped the phone tighter. "When he drove me away from you that nightmarish evening ten years ago, he took me home to pack my things before driving me to Switzerland.

"My mother helped me and packed my winter coat I would need later. She told me she'd sewn a lot of money she'd been secretly earning and saving into the lining along with my birth certificate and a letter I should read. Maman said she would send me a birthday present by Christmas with a hidden message so I could escape because I wasn't safe from my father."

"You have an amazing mother, Fleurine."

"I know. Later that very night he drove me to his older sister's house in Souboz, Switzerland, to that offshoot cult neighborhood he'd come from. His plan was to force me to marry the son of one of his cult friends as soon as I turned eighteen. I had to stay his sister's prisoner for four months. As you know, I turned eighteen the day before Christmas and had the legal right to leave. The next day I ran away."

He made a sound like he'd been shot. "Fleurine—"

"Please hear me out. When a neighbor came over to talk to my aunt on Christmas night for a few minutes, I climbed out a second-story window and across the icy roof. I had to jump into a snow-filled wagon. All I had on was my coat over my dress. When no one was around, I started running in my brown shoes, praying I wouldn't get caught. If I did, I prayed to die."

"This sounds so incredible!"

"It *was*!" Her voice caught. "The birthday present Maman had sent me was an alpine hat with a message and some more money fastened inside the wide band. She told me to run away and never come back because my father would never stop looking for me or you.

"Maman said my father had you under constant surveillance no matter where you went or what you did. That terrified me, but I was thankful she'd given me my passport to freedom with that money and birth certificate."

Her mother had also given her advice about

never depending on a man for anything. Most women did that and came to grief like she had. Fleurine needed to depend on herself from now on. It was the only way to have a life. But that was thinking that she didn't share with Raoul.

"How did you manage?" The tremor in his voice shook her.

"I'd planned for my escape during those four months, procured a passport and caught a train leaving for Paris. Once there, I asked a traveler's-aid person at the station where I could find a cheap rooming house. She gave me directions. I took a taxi there and stayed under the new name I'd given myself. The next day I bought a blouse and skirt and normal shoes, then I looked for work."

"This is unbelievable."

"Looking back, it sounds that way to me too. I remembered what you'd said about my baking. I found a job at a bakery near the rooming house. When I told the owner I could make *mannele*, I was given a chance to prove it. He liked the chocolate bits on top, and I ended up getting the job."

She heard his sharp intake of breath. "You're absolutely amazing."

"No. Just desperate. I asked the shady guy working in the back where I could find someone to make me a new legal birth certificate."

"What did he want in return?" The savage tone in his voice made her shiver.

"I paid him my first month's wages so he wouldn't tell anyone."

"And he took it," Raoul bit out.

"Yes. I didn't care. I now had the legal name Laure Millet on that document. My father wouldn't be able to trace me. Pretty soon the owner was letting me prepare all the bread recipes I'd learned from my mother, and my salary increased substantially.

"I worked there full-time until fall. At that point I'd saved enough money to start my studies at the university to become a computer science engineer. I went to classes while working part-time. Five years ago I graduated, found a suitable apartment and got the job at Aire-Tech."

"You've left me speechless."

"I've done too much talking and hope you'll be able to forgi—"

"Look." He broke in on her. "I can't handle all this over the phone. We need to talk in person."

"We mustn't."

"Before you tell me no, I have an idea. I'm staying at the *palais* right now. I've told you about it before. These days it's being used to house vets and a lot of maintenance is going on. So here's what we're going to do."

"Wait—"

"Please let me finish, Fleurine. We've used the same painting firm for years and they're working on one of the suites right now. Tomorrow I'll have two of the female workers come to your apartment in a small van from *Adolphe Entreprise de Peinture*. Its logo is on the side.

"One of them will let you put on her uniform, and you'll leave with the driver, fully disguised. The other woman will wait ten minutes then go. I'll be in my suite when you reach the *palais*. Guy, the man at the entrance, will show you the elevator to my suite. Whoever is tailing me won't have a clue about you. What's your address?"

"Stop, Raoul. It's too dangerous."

"Then, I'll get your address another way. Be prepared to open your apartment door at eight in the morning. I'll be waiting for you at the *palais*."

"Wait—don't hang up!" she cried. "Since you're insisting, here's the address." She gave it to him. "I live in an apartment above a two-car garage next to the home of the owner. I'll leave the garage door open. When they drive in, I'll close it, and they can come up the interior stairs. No one will know what's going on."

"Perfect."

"Except for one thing." She took a steadying breath. "Don't underestimate my father. He's looking for me with a special vengeance. When I ran away from my aunt's, another sin had been committed in his eyes. He'd promised to make me the wife of his friend's son, the one I supposedly married. My escape deepened his rage. He never forgives or forgets."

"Neither do I, Fleurine. Neither do I…"

CHAPTER THREE

SATURDAY MORNING COULDN'T come soon enough for Raoul who'd tossed and turned all night. That monster Garber had played him and Fleurine with the master touch.

Spreading the lie on the estate that Fleurine had been married all this time had been the Dumotte coup de grâce. From the very beginning no one had questioned his colossal prevarication that prevented Raoul from trying to find Fleurine. The man's evil soul had no equal.

Showered and shaved, Raoul dressed in the same kind of jeans and T-shirt he'd worn on the estate in his teens. While he waited, he made coffee. Earlier he'd asked for fruit and ham and cheese croissants to be brought from the kitchen.

It was ten after nine. Too impatient to wait any longer, he walked through the suite to the foyer. He was about to take the elevator down to the main floor when the door opened. His heart slammed into his throat to see five-foot-seven Fleurine looking adorable in her disguise. Yet no cap or overalls could hide her dazzling violet eyes and beauty from his gaze.

"Thank you for coming, Fleurine. I know this has taken courage." His gaze fused with hers. "I'm still trying to grasp the fact that you've been in Paris all these years and were never married." His hands curled into fists. "If I'd had any idea…"

"It had to be that way. My father is a monster, Raoul, and his diabolical propaganda did exactly what he'd intended it to do. Your father stole the woman he loved away from him. In return he made certain I could never be with you. In his cruelty, he found the perfect way to keep us apart and hold my mother hostage.

"Among the other things she wrote to me, she admitted that if she told the truth to anyone else, he would kill her and my siblings." Fleurine's eyes reflected a world of pain.

"His threat succeeded," Raoul ground out. "But we have your mother to thank for keeping her silence. You and I are still breathing and together again. Let's celebrate that much, at least. Why don't you come into my lair and we'll get you out of that disguise, fetching as it is."

That sweet smile he'd loved broke the tension. She followed him into the salon, removing the cap that released her luscious hair. Next, she undid the overalls and stepped out of them, revealing her gorgeous figure.

Raoul picked up both items and put them on a chair. It was still incredible to see her in anything but a white dress. Today she'd worn stylish tan pleated pants and a short-sleeved crewneck aqua top. His gaze wandered over her. "I feel like we're in a time warp."

"Maybe we are." Her eyes had filmed over.

"All these years I've imagined you living in Switzerland with some deranged man your father picked out from their cult. Someone who treated you the way your father treats your mother as long as she behaves."

She shuddered. "Thank heaven for my mother who made it possible for me to escape before his cohorts trapped me for good."

"Amen," he said in a thick voice. "You look

a little unsteady, Fleurine. Sit down on the couch, and I'll bring us coffee and food."

"I could use some." She sank down on the end of it.

"Du sucre? De la crème?"

"Both. Thank you."

He hurried into the kitchen and came back with their mugs and a plate of croissants and fruit. After he set everything on the coffee table, she reached for a mug and started sipping the hot liquid. "Oh, this tastes good."

Raoul sat in a chair across from her and began drinking his. "You'll like the croissants, but I'd rather devour…" He was about to say he wanted to devour her. "I'd give anything for some of your *mannele*. They were to die for."

Her mouth curved in remembrance of that moment in the hay barn when he'd devoured the one she'd made for him. She sat back and crossed her elegant legs, looking relaxed. "I've seen your picture in the paper and on TV. The news of your brothers' marriages made the front page of a dozen newspapers and tabloids across France. I've kept expecting to see your wedding announced at some point. Are you secretly married, and the intrusive reporters haven't found out about it yet? I promise I won't tell."

Her question threw him off guard. This teasing, more assertive side of Fleurine was so different from the vulnerable girl he'd loved he was incredulous. But he had to remember that seventeen-year-old Fleurine had never been allowed access to the media or newspapers.

Hers had been an isolated world until she'd run away from all that. Since then, she'd been living in the modern world and was a brilliant software engineer. The change in her shouldn't have surprised him, but it did. He'd been living in the past too long.

"I'm still single like you, Fleurine. But it's taking me time to comprehend that over all these years, *you've* been living in Paris and never were married. That engineer Paul I met last evening appeared so protective of you I couldn't help but wonder if he's someone special to you." If they were in a relationship, that might explain his strange behavior toward Raoul.

She shook her head. "He's a recent hire. Nothing more."

Her clipped answer relieved him, yet he

could tell she was holding something back. The teenage Fleurine who'd opened her heart to him—the girl he'd known and adored— seemed to have disappeared. Her whole demeanor was different. "I want to know details of what happened to you after your father drove you away from the barn."

He heard her take a deep breath. "Because I was on the other side of the truck, you wouldn't have known I got sick to my stomach. When I finally climbed inside, I felt more dead than alive."

"That describes me, not only then, but for many years after."

"I hear you, but I want to know about you." Again, their gazes caught. "Did you leave for Paris the next day?"

He nodded. "With my brothers. We flew here and settled in our suites. This one has always been mine. It became my study hall for four years until I graduated in business administration along with Nic. At that point Papa put us in charge of running some of the businesses for the company."

She reached for a croissant. "What about Jean-Louis?"

"He'd never wanted to leave the estate."

"I remember he was always working in the garage after school."

"That's my brother. He couldn't take Paris or the studying, so he dropped out of school after a few weeks. The next thing we knew he'd joined the army under an assumed name. He disappeared, and we didn't see him again until this last June after we hired a private detective to find him."

Her eyes widened. "He's been gone ten years too?"

"He wanted a different life. Losing him and you within a month did a lot of damage to me. It's a long story, but now he's home and married. So is Nic, as you have discovered in the news. They both oversee special projects and live on the estate as I do. Everything has changed because Papa had to retire."

"*Your* father retired? I didn't know that."

"He has heart disease, but we never allowed his retirement to be made public. My cousin Pascal and his co-CEO, George Delong, have been quietly running Causcelle since then. This is where you come in, Fleurine."

"What do you mean?"

"They're on the verge of buying Rayonner-

Tech for the corporation. I was asked to sit in on the interview when their CEO, Jules Vaugier, talked to you. Pascal wanted my opinion of the software engineer Jules might hire before he and George acquired that company."

She stirred. "So *that's* how it happened. I know they questioned my lack of experience. Now it all makes sense why you were brought in. Little did you know I'd turn out to be Fleur Dumotte in disguise."

Fleurine, Fleurine. Where have you gone?

Though he found pure pleasure in just looking at her again, this new layer of sophistication and attitude she displayed troubled him because it didn't seem real. "I'd like to think fate decided it was time to bring us together."

"Our meeting should never have happened." Her flat statement minus any emotion startled him. "When the receptionist told me your name and said that you were in the conference room waiting for the interview to start, you can't imagine my terror."

"Obviously not."

"The second I heard your name, I tripped and fell. In that instant I had to make up a story to get out of the building before you saw me. I knew you were being watched, and I feared a catastrophe would occur the second we were caught together."

Raoul took a quick breath, trying to figure out this version of Fleurine. He understood the fear part, but not her pragmatic, detached aloofness so unlike the loving, sensitive girl who'd won his heart. "Both Jules and I were surprised when we heard what happened in the foyer."

"I had to do something so you wouldn't see me, but I hated taking up Monsieur Vaugier's valuable time."

If Raoul didn't know better, he could almost believe another woman inhabited Fleurine's body at this moment. She didn't sound like his childhood sweetheart. "You don't need to be concerned about that."

"But I am, of course," she asserted.

He finished his coffee. "I phoned him later to let him know you were all right."

"That was kind of you, Raoul. You always were the perfect gentleman. But after this experience, I've ruined my chances to interview with him."

Wait—it was *that* important to her? Nothing could have pained him more. "That's not true. I'm your advocate and will arrange another interview if that's what you wish. I'd do anything for you."

Fleurine shook her head, hurting him more. "You're sweet, but I wouldn't expect that, Raoul. In truth I've changed my mind about that job."

What?

"Tell me something. Is your Oncle Raimond still running the estate?"

Now she'd changed the subject.

Fleurine...what's going on with you?

"He died four months ago."

"Oh, I'm sorry. Then, who's running things now?"

He rubbed the back of his neck. "*I* am."

She put down her mug. "*You* are the head of everything there now and still do business in Paris?"

"When necessary. Papa put me in charge when he retired."

"Does that mean you know where my father is and what he's been doing? I know nothing."

Clearly her fear of her father was real, but where was her interest in the love they'd once shared? "I know a lot."

Fleurine jumped to her feet. "Did he force my mother and family to live in Souboz? Do you know how she is? Anything? Since I left for Paris, it's been the greatest pain of my life not being able to see or talk to her, never knowing anything."

But you haven't been in pain over me?

This was a nightmare. His stomach muscles clenched. "Relax. Your whole family is still living on the estate in the home where you were born."

"Thank heaven!" she cried.

"We don't talk, but I see them every once in a while. She and your siblings are fine."

"I'm so thankful for that, but where's my father?"

Raoul stood up, knowing in his gut she wouldn't like his answer. "He's living right there with your family and still runs the dairy."

"No!" Her pained cry reverberated in the room.

She spun around as tears gushed down her cheeks that had suddenly paled. The real Fleurine had broken through for a moment. "I don't believe it! Why did you never tell your father what my father did to us so he could at least be thrown off the estate?"

He understood that anguish. "I could ask you a similar question. When you fled to Paris, why didn't you tell the police what happened on that horrific evening?"

"Because my mother had sworn me to secrecy and had a plan for my escape. I didn't want to go against her for fear of her life."

His insides twisted. "That's my answer too. I didn't dare reveal what he'd done for fear of retaliation that could end in bloodshed. We knew your father hated mine. If he had brought a criminal lawsuit against Garber for threatening us at the point of a rifle, all hell would have broken loose, and you know it."

She moaned. "But with you in charge, I still don't understand how you can stand to allow my father to remain on the property after what happened."

"Think about it, Fleurine. His crimes were against the Church as well as humanity. The knowledge of what he and his cohorts did to those monks could cause a conflict of national proportions, let alone to your family."

A shudder ran through her. "You're right. My father is a vile criminal, and he has hired men to spy on you all these years. This simply has to end for all our sakes!" she cried.

"Understand one thing, Fleurine. I may be the head of the estate, but it's still my father's decision. Your father has always done his job well and knows how to run the dairy. If I were to fire him, Papa would have to know the reason. Once he heard the whole truth—including your father's part in the monks' deaths—his heart would give out on the spot. I couldn't bear to be the one to bring on a fatal attack."

She hugged her waist. "Naturally you couldn't let that happen." Her voice trembled. "But don't forget my father would kill us right now if he saw us together."

"Let's view this a different way. Nothing bad has happened yet. Furthermore, your mother has never gone to the authorities with proof of what she knows. It would take her coming forward for him to be imprisoned, but she never has. Instead, she has stayed with him and made the best of a ghastly situation to protect and take care of your siblings. She helped you get away because she knew he hated me for loving you."

Fleurine looked devastated. "That's true, and she won me my freedom, thus preventing *your* murder so far. What you're saying is that she's a saint, and she is, but it's so horribly wrong! I can't stand that she still lives with that monster. My poor brother and sister. They're terrified of him. It isn't right they have to live under his edicts for the rest of their lives. It isn't fair what he's done to you and your family, Raoul!"

He could tell she was at the breaking point and pulled her sobbing body into his arms, aching to comfort her. For the next few minutes, he rocked her, kissing her wet face until she started to quiet down.

"Then, it's time we ended his tyranny for good. Now that we both know the whole truth, we can change everything. Here's what is going to happen."

"No, Raoul! *We're* not going to do anything."

In a decisive move that stunned him, Fleurine broke free of his arms and put distance between them. "I ran away from my father. That part was my fault and put your life in danger. You're a Causcelle who would fight to the death against cruelty. But this is one fight that will result in the loss of both our lives. I refuse to allow that to happen."

He watched her pull the overalls over her

lovely body and sweep her hair up under the cap. "You can't leave yet. We haven't begun to talk about *us*." He was dying to kiss her and never let her go.

Her eyes flashed. "There's no *us*, Raoul! Don't you get it? Now that we both know exactly where he is and what he's been doing, the knowledge makes our lives worse than ever. Nothing has changed in ten years. You and I could still be seventeen and eighteen, my father's pawns. But by some miracle we're both still walking and functioning. Let's keep it that way."

"Fleurine—"

"We have nothing to talk about. We never did because we were children. Go back to your life I've seen on the news. Most men would give their souls to lead the life of Raoul Causcelle. *Femmes d'Aujourd'hui* voted you the most desirable man in Europe. Wow!

"While you enjoy that life, I'm going back to mine as a software engineer. I love it, and right now I'm headed downstairs to find the other painter. She'll drive me back to my apartment, and this will be the end of it."

She pivoted and hurried to the elevator in the foyer. Raoul didn't try to detain her. Fleurine wasn't herself. He'd decided she was in shock. So was he. How did you process ten years' worth of unknown information in one fell swoop?

He reeled with exultation. She wasn't married, and knowing the full truth had set them both free at last. Her father could no longer stop them from finding their way back to each other now. He would see to it.

By the time the elevator door closed, Raoul was already working on a plan in his mind to take care of her father so they could be together. Within a few weeks he'd be able to put it into action. Best of all, Fleurine wouldn't be going anywhere. He knew exactly where to find her.

Three weeks later on a Monday morning, Fleurine knocked on her CEO's open door. "*Bonjour*, Philippe."

"Oh, good, Laure. You're here. Come in."

Fleurine walked into his office, fearing he knew about her visit to Rayonner-Tech three weeks ago. No doubt he'd called her in for an explanation. Paul had been in her office when the police had talked to her. She imagined that because she'd hurt him, he would tell their boss everything he'd overheard. Philippe would probably let her go.

All Fleurine could depend on was herself and her education. If she lost this job at Aire-Tech, she would find another one. She was sorry about it, because Philippe had been such a wonderful employer. Never would she have considered a move if it hadn't been for Paul.

Fleurine sat down in front of his desk. "Bruno saw me as I came in from the parking lot and said you were looking for me. I witnessed a car accident on my way here and had to give the police a statement. That's why I'm late."

"Was anyone hurt?"

"No, thank heaven."

"That's good. It's an odd coincidence that you would mention police."

Oh, no—he *did* know what had happened three weeks ago.

Philippe smiled. "Over the weekend I had a conference call with the chief of police in Nice on the Côte d'Azur. He'd been talking to the chief of police here in Paris. The man told him about the terrific job *you* did solving a serious problem with their department's computer system last year. Your fame has been spreading."

What? "I don't understand."

"He wanted to know if you were available to sort out some problems for them since their move to another part of Nice. He estimates it could take a week."

Wait—had she just heard him correctly? Philippe *wasn't* terminating her? That meant Paul hadn't said anything yet. He was probably still holding out hope to get together with her. *Never.*

"You mean you want to send me to Nice on a job?"

He nodded. "Not if you don't want to or can't. They need an expert. I told him they wouldn't find anyone better than you. Would that be a problem for you?"

"Of course not. I'm just…surprised." Shocked. Dumbfounded. For seventeen years she'd never been anywhere but on the estate. After a brief four months in the Jura mountains of Souboz, Switzerland, she'd spent the rest of her life in Paris. She'd never traveled anywhere, let alone been on a jet.

"It's a compliment to you and our company, my dear. There's a big bonus involved. What's your schedule like?"

She needed to get hold of herself. "I'll be finishing up at the Guerlain Institute by tomorrow."

"Then, can I tell him you'll fly down on Wednesday? They'll pay for your flight and hotel accommodations while you're there."

"Yes! I'm thrilled for the opportunity and would like to go." Since walking out of Raoul's suite three weeks ago, Fleurine had made up her mind to move on with her life. He belonged in the distant past, and his world could never be hers. Her mother had been right about that.

"My secretary will supply you with the details at the end of your workday tomorrow."

"Thank you for everything, Philippe."

Fleurine got up from the chair and left his office slightly dazed by this unexpected turn of events. This job opportunity couldn't have come at a more propitious moment.

A week away from Paul would be a blessing she hadn't expected. It would also give her time to look into job opportunities elsewhere if Paul continued to harass her after she returned.

Raoul was another matter. She'd been forced to live with the pain of losing him years ago. It had been clear from the start that their relationship had been doomed. Nothing had changed since then. Her father was still front and center. Garber Dumotte, the monster, would always be on the hunt for the two of them and a danger to her mom and siblings.

Thankfully Raoul had gotten the message to leave it alone and hadn't called her since she'd left his suite at the *palais*. That was because they'd both grown up and changed. In truth, they weren't in love. Not anymore. For a decade their lives had been on different paths. He had one destiny. She had another. Except that wasn't completely true. She'd never stopped loving him and never would. He would always be her heart's desire, which made it imperative she push him away to keep them both safe.

Raoul might not be married, but he was an important man in the business world. The news featured him with many beautiful women. It crushed her every time she saw his picture or an article about him.

As for Fleurine, she had a wonderful career

and friends and looked forward to all the new opportunities ahead of her. Maybe there'd be a special man one day, but she couldn't imagine it.

This trip to the South of France would give her a change of scenery. She needed a diversion before she had to face Paul again. One more difficult confrontation with him and she would leave Aire-Tech without hesitation.

CHAPTER FOUR

ON TUESDAY EVENING after work, Fleurine had to call Deline and cancel their plans to go to a film. She'd needed time to get packed. She would call her when she returned from the job she had to do in Nice for Aire-Tech. They chatted for a few more minutes. Deline had sounded excited for her after learning it would be her first flight. Fleurine wasn't so sure about it before they said goodbye.

Philippe's secretary had laid out the plans for her. She was ready Wednesday morning wearing a three-piece apricot suit when a taxi came to take her to Charles de Gaulle Airport. After a flight to Nice first class, a police escort would pick her up and drive her to her hotel.

Fleurine hadn't known what to expect, but her nervousness subsided once the jet gained altitude in a sea of blue September sky. To think her mother and family would never have an experience like this...

She felt an acute loneliness as she noticed the number of couples on the flight. Fleurine had a feeling that one of them seated in front of her was on their *lune de miel*. She could only wonder what it would be like to honeymoon with her own husband. With Raoul. No one else.

Only once years ago in the hay barn with Raoul had she experienced moments of pure joy and the fleeting promise of marriage in their nonexistent future. Perhaps another good man might come into her life one day. She couldn't imagine it. There was only one Raoul. If it didn't happen, she'd take her mother's wisdom to heart. Millions of happy women were fulfilled without a man.

Later, during the descent, the view of the coastal city with its elegant bay and palm trees at the foot of the Alps amazed her. Once they'd landed on the runway, the jet eventually taxied to a stop. Fleurine filed out with the other passengers. Two police officers approached her, staring at her with decidedly masculine interest.

"Mademoiselle Laure Millet from Aire-

Tech?" She nodded. "We're Officers Bernard and Tremblay, asked to meet you and take you to Cagnes-sur-Mer."

"I was told I'd be met by the police, but I thought I'd be working in Nice."

"You're needed in Cagnes-sur-Mer first. It's a town close to Nice."

"Oh, well, thank you very much."

"If you'll follow us to that helicopter over there."

She saw it in the distance and clutched her purse in reaction. "Can't we just drive there?"

"The helicopter is faster and avoids traffic, unless that makes you uncomfortable."

Instead of a woman of the world, Fleurine felt like a fool. "I'm sure it will be fine. It's just that I've never been on one before." A helicopter was so different from a huge jet.

"You'll like it a lot."

"What about my suitcase?"

"Lieutenant Bernard will bring it to the helicopter."

"Thank you. It's a jade-colored spinner with my name on the tag."

"He'll find it. If you'll come with me."

While one officer went in search of her luggage, Fleurine followed this one across

the tarmac to a gleaming white-and-blue helicopter. A man inside opened the door for
her to board.

"Mademoiselle Millet?" the officer said.
"I'll leave you in the hands of your pilot, Yves
Cervaine. This will be her first time, Yves."

What? She turned to her escort in surprise.
"You're not coming?"

"If you're comfortable taking the helicopter, Officer Bernard and I will answer another
call that just came in, but he'll be here with
your bag momentarily. Be assured you'll be
greeted when you arrive in Cagnes-sur-Mer."

"Of course. Thank you for meeting me."

"It's been our pleasure."

As he walked away, she climbed on board.
The pilot told her to sit behind him and fasten
her seat belt. "I'll be gentle. It's only a short
flight, and I'm sure you'll enjoy it." He put
on his headgear.

"I'm sure I will." Again, she was irritated
at herself for being so nervous and tried to
act nonchalant. Thousands of people did this
every day.

She looked around the elegant white interior, noticing it had three seats on each
side and picture windows. This had to be the

height of luxury, something she'd never experienced. From her window she took in a partial view of Nice. The city seemed larger than she'd imagined with its hilly landscape and beaches lapped by the Mediterranean.

While Fleurine watched another jet land, she heard men's voices. The officer must have come with her suitcase. She was still staring out the window when the door closed. To her surprise he came in and sat down opposite her. She turned to him, wondering why the officer hadn't joined his partner.

"Raoul!" Her cry rang out. She felt as if she were going to faint.

"Relax, Fleurine. Please hear me out. Before we go anywhere, this is a chance for us to reconnect. I won't force you to go against your will, but I would like very much if you accepted. Surely after ten years you didn't think our meeting at the *palais* would be the end of everything." His deep voice curled to her insides. "The truth is, there is no job."

Her breath caught. Another lie, but Raoul had been the author of this one.

"Your boss doesn't know that," he enlightened her. "The beauty of it is that you've been given a whole week off. Nic and Jean-Louis are taking over for me on the estate so I can have a week's vacation too."

With those revelations, realization dawned. She wasn't sitting across from just any man in this helicopter. This was a breathtaking, black-haired Adonis with unfathomable money, connections and the means to do anything he wanted, anytime. He still didn't understand the danger he was in, but she knew there'd be a horrible price to pay for this.

"You know you're being followed? And have you forgotten my mother and siblings are at risk?"

"They're the reason I haven't been able to come to you before now. Since we've been apart, I've arranged to keep them safe. I swear it. Don't be afraid, Fleurine. Nothing's going to happen to anyone. Believe me when I tell you I've provided all of us protection."

Fleurine would always believe him, but she was terrified and struggled to swallow.

"Will you at least give us the time to talk things over in favorable surroundings? It's up to you. If you want to fly back to Paris right now on the Causcelle jet, you can. Or you can come with me so we can discuss the situation in more depth before we part company for good. After ten years apart, we need this time. What's your answer?"

Her answer would be to fling herself into his arms. Barring that, she would agree to go with him because she loved and trusted him. "I'll come if we're not gone long."

"Thank you, Fleurine." He told Yves to start up the helicopter.

Between the shock of seeing him and the sound of the rotors whining, any more words caught in her throat. Again, she felt like she was going to faint.

While he fastened his seat belt, she took in the gorgeous sight of him dressed in casual white trousers and an open-necked hunter-green sport shirt. Those black orbs studied every inch of her, igniting flares of awareness she couldn't prevent from exploding throughout her body. She loved him so desperately. She clutched the armrests as the helicopter rose in the air.

While they passed over the landscape below, her sanity started to return and, with it, her fear. Her emotions were spilling all over the place, but she fought to maintain her composure in front of him.

* * *

Raoul studied her profile. "We're headed for the island of Ischia. It's one of my favorite seaside resorts in Italy that isn't yet overrun with every tourist on the planet. We'll be staying at a friend's villa and will be there soon. I'd planned to take you there on our honeymoon, but we know what interfered with those dreams. Today I can promise you nothing will interrupt our pleasure on this trip."

Right now, Fleurine was too upset to talk. He eyed the woman he loved, pained because she'd lived her whole life in fear. Growing up with a father like Garber shouldn't happen to any child. Raoul had talked to Father Didier at the church in La Racineuse about his love for Fleurine and the pain she and her family were still forced to endure.

The priest had had to remind him that Garber had once been a good little boy who'd grown up in a dysfunctional family belonging to a cult.

What Raoul needed to do was be a loving support to Fleurine and earn her trust before he did anything else.

That's what Raoul hoped to accomplish this trip. While they were together, he'd tell her about the steps he'd taken to ensure everyone's safety. In time there'd be more information forthcoming to set her at ease because this was only the beginning, and he'd never let her go.

By three o'clock, the pilot set them down on the pad at the rear of a private villa made of stone tucked in greenery and flowers. After Raoul helped her out of the helicopter with her suitcase, he walked her around where a handsome older couple came out to greet them, first in Italian, then French.

Raoul hugged both of them, then turned to her. "Fleurine Dumotte, I want you to meet Genevra and Alonzo Romano, my parents' best friends from years ago. They're my favorite people too."

Raoul had been planning all this while Fleurine had assumed she'd seen the very last of him. She was still trying to comprehend everything going on before she looked up at him. "They knew your mother?"

His vibrant black eyes searched hers. "It's why I've liked to vacation here over the years when I've been able. I love hearing about her.

Genevra tells me things that make Maman live for me. I love her and Alonzo."

"I can see why." She turned to their hosts, unable to prevent her eyes from misting over. "This is the most beautiful place I've ever seen in my life. All the flowers and that dazzling blue Mediterranean. I've never lived near water. Thank you for letting me be a guest here."

Genevra took her arm. "While Raoul talks to Alonzo, let me show you to your room where you can freshen up. We haven't seen him for at least six months."

Try ten years.

Fleurine followed her through the charming villa to a bedroom with its en suite bathroom and a terrace. Someone on their staff had already brought in her suitcase and put it on a bench at the end of the double bed.

"We want you and Raoul to relax and do whatever you like. I miss all of Delphine and Louis's children, but this one has been sad for many years. Today some of that sadness is gone. I think I know why." Her brown eyes twinkled before she kissed Fleurine's cheek.

The older woman's words touched her deeply. If Raoul had been sad all these years, had he been thinking about Fleurine, longing for her as she had for him? But maybe that was foolish to believe when he was constantly photographed with beautiful women on his arm. For all she knew he'd gotten close to one special woman after all this time.

"Do you know the boys look the most like their mother? She was a dark-haired beauty who bewitched men everywhere. But the only man she ever could see was her handsome Louis, who was a wonder in his own right."

Fleurine knew all about that from her own mother. Delphine Ronfleur had bewitched Louis Causcelle and had unconsciously cast a spell on Fleurine's father, but she didn't want to think about that right now.

"Those triplet sons turned out to be the most beautiful boys imaginable. For my best friend to have died giving birth to them will always be my greatest sorrow. Now they're too handsome for their own good, as you have found out."

"I and all the girls." Fleurine nodded. "I grew up on the Causcelle estate and have known Raoul and his brothers since we were little children. As he got older, he reminded me of a dashing pirate."

Genevra laughed softly. "He's that, all right, and you—like his mother—had to be the most beautiful girl on the estate. It's the reason why Raoul has brought you here and never took his eyes off you out there." The other woman saw what she wanted to see because she didn't know what was really going on.

"How did your two families meet?"

"Alonzo and I got to know them right after they were married and vacationing here in Ischia. We'd just been married too, and all four of us were still in our late teens. While Alonzo and I were out fishing, we met Louis and Delphine at the same spot and started talking. My husband ran his father's business, as did Louis. Both men had a lot in common and struck up a lasting friendship.

"Delphine and I were so much alike we became friends overnight. We became pregnant around the same times with our first three. I had two girls and a boy. She had three girls. Then came three boys she would never see." Her eyes filled with tears. "Before they were born, she had dreams for her triplets to help their father in business and support him after all his hard work."

Fleurine's eyes smarted. "What a tragedy she died."

"It was, and so very hard on Louis. But he rose to the occasion in a most magnificent way. Six children to raise on his own with all his tremendous responsibilities. Thousands of people throughout France have relied on his leadership and generosity for years. He's a saint. We've been to see him recently. It's a miracle he's still alive considering his bad heart."

Until three weeks ago, Fleurine hadn't known anything about Louis Causcelle. Hearing Genevra's loving defense of him made her ashamed of her outburst on that last day with Raoul at the *palais*. The reason why Louis had never known what Fleurine's father had done to her and Raoul was because Raoul had wanted to protect his father from too much pain.

Fleurine was also ashamed for having nursed a resentment against Raoul's father for making him and his brothers go to college in Paris. She'd felt at the time he'd been too strict with his boys. His father had taken Raoul away from her. This woman's revelations helped her see things clearly, including Fleurine's selfishness and immaturity at seventeen.

She understood Raoul's reasoning now and his wisdom. She also understood something else. Raoul had believed Fleurine had been married all those years. In order to keep her and her family safe, he'd never done anything to find her. Raoul was made of the true stuff of heroes. She would always revere him, but that time had passed for both of them and couldn't be recovered.

Fleurine put a hand on Genevra's arm. "You won't understand this, but I'm grateful to you for everything you've told me. It has answered some questions for me, and I can't thank you enough for confiding in me. It's no wonder you and the Causcelles gravitated to each other years ago. Raoul told me he feels closer to his mother when he's here. You're an angel yourself."

As she leaned over to kiss the older woman's cheek, Raoul walked in the bedroom. "Is everything all right, you two?"

A smile broke out on Genevra's face. "Everything is perfect when *you* come for a visit, *mon fils*. Your bedroom is ready for you downstairs."

The woman had a special spot in her heart for Raoul to call him her son. "Now, I'm going to find my husband, and I'll see that your dinner will be served whenever you're ready." She kissed his cheek and left.

Suddenly Fleurine realized they were alone and in a bedroom. How many times in the past had she dreamed of a situation like this where they could give in to their desire? But this was no fantasy trip, and it was ten years later. They were strangers now, never destined to be one.

As her mother had written on that message long ago:

You and Raoul were born into separate worlds. You were never meant to step out of them to be together. Remember that a woman can be fulfilled and successful without a man.

Even if danger from her father weren't a factor, Fleurine's hopes for them had died in the past.

Fleurine was a twenty-eight-year-old career woman at this point, no longer a starry-eyed teenager. Looking at life honestly, she could never hope to be with a man like Raoul. They weren't from the same class of people. That old cliché that water and oil don't mix rang true in their case. Raoul would never marry a software engineer, of all people. The thought was ridiculous.

"Genevra is wonderful, Raoul. She loves you."

"It's mutual, and from my vantage point, she's taken with you."

"She's made me very comfortable, but this isn't my reality. I flew down here thinking I had a job to do, but all this—"

"Is just too much?" he finished for her.

She stared at him. "In all honesty, I'm thrilled to see you again in person and know that you are well. But I need to get back to the work I love."

Something flickered in the recesses of his eyes. "Why don't you change into something comfortable, Fleurine? When you're ready, join me on your terrace where we can talk as long as we want. Take your time."

"I'll be right out." She moved past him and went inside to the bathroom where she could freshen up. Raoul believed he could triumph over Garber Dumotte. Unfortunately, her mentally ill father would continue to be relentless in tracking him.

As Genevra had said, the triplets had inherited their mother's looks. Every time her father saw Raoul, he imagined the woman he'd never had a chance to love, all because of Louis Causcelle. Fleurine had always known what she had to do to prevent a disaster. It had meant never being with Raoul again.

If only she hadn't applied for that position at Rayonner-Tech…

Fleurine had unwittingly set wheels in motion that had brought Raoul back into her world. Only he with his Causcelle connections could have planned a secret rendezvous to get them back together. But rather than be upset about it, she realized this trip to Ischia *was* giving them a chance to say a real goodbye.

With her mind made up, she refreshed her lipstick. He would always be the most desirable man alive, but she couldn't give in to momentary pleasure. She'd meant it when she'd told him she wanted to go her own way. Fleurine needed to be in charge of her life while her father was still alive and free to commit mayhem. Raoul had also been leading his own full life for years. From everything she'd read about him in the newspapers and seen on TV, he'd been enjoying his bachelor status since his university days.

Forget the belated honeymoon he'd imagined here in Ischia. It would never happen because she and Raoul weren't meant to be together.

One day Raoul would get used to seeing Fleurine in a modern-day wardrobe. But when she first walked out on the terrace in a luscious pink top and tan capri pants a few minutes later, he had to purposely erase his earlier vision of her in eighteenth-century garb.

She smiled. "Why are you staring?"

"You're a stunning woman."

"But?"

"I don't want to say something that will bring back bad memories for you."

"You mean of always seeing the pathetic girl in white?" Fleurine could read his mind. She sat down on a chair opposite him at the patio table. "After I escaped, it took me a year to accept the fact that I could resemble a twentieth-century French girl. I used to look in the rooming-house mirror at the new clothes I was wearing and think it was some kind of trick."

He cocked his dark head. "I'm going to let you in on a secret. The face and long flowing hair above the dress enchanted me from day one. Those white dresses couldn't hide your gorgeous figure. In fact, they made you more alluring, even with those brown ankle shoes your father forced you to wear. You always stood out, like the violets in the pasture that reminded me of your exquisite eyes."

"I had no idea."

"Forgive me if I've embarrassed you, Fleurine, but you have to know how attractive you always were and are. Why do you think Thomas and Remy followed you around with their tongues hanging out?"

"If they did, I didn't notice."

"They weren't the only ones. Every guy at the school wanted a chance with you, but they were too terrified of your father."

"That didn't stop you."

"No, because I had help. Oncle Raimond ran the estate. He knew how I felt about you, and he told me to waylay you at the north pasture after school on your way home. It was the one time of day when he arranged for your father to visit the other farms."

"He actually did that?" The news shocked and delighted her.

"Even if our meetings had to be out in the open, we got lucky for a long time."

"Until—"

"Let's not go there. We're here now. It's time for you to know what I've done to keep all of us safe."

She leaned forward. "As long as my father is alive, we can never be seen together."

"That's where you're wrong. I have the best minds in the country working on our problem."

"It won't work, Raoul."

"The day I left your office, I had the security guards at the *palais* watch to see if I was being followed. We went through the surveillance-camera footage that covered the last three months and discovered one man who shouldn't have been driving in and out at all hours. The police traced the plate to a man who lives and works in Paris."

Fleurine gasped quietly. "I knew it."

"This is only the beginning. After you left my suite wearing your disguise, I set up a meeting with two men to devise a plan. George Delong is the co-CEO with my cousin Pascal, but he's also a brilliant attorney who helped my father rise to power. He knows the ins and outs of the law.

"The other man, Claude Giraud, is the former secret-service agent who worked for the last president of France. He's the one who found Jean-Louis for our family. The two men have contacts and inside connections with police and judges that reach everywhere. Between their findings, we've already taken steps to tie your father's hands."

She shook her head. "I don't see how."

"With that license plate lead, they got a warrant to tap the man's phone and that of your father."

After a long silence she said, "That's incredible."

"At that point they discovered that your father is in constant contact with him. He's the one being paid to follow me. When I'm in the city, he tails me and reports back to your father. That man is called Franz Brust. Does that name ring any bells?"

"Yes. *He* was one of those teenage guys from Switzerland my father ran around with.

He works with my father in the dairy on the estate. Maman couldn't stand him."

"Well, it appears your father moved him to Paris, and he works at the Causcelle cheese outlet watching my every move when I'm there."

"Maman spoke the truth, didn't she?"

"There's more. Do you remember a local farmer, Ernst Keller?"

He saw her shudder. "Keller was also part of that teenage gang from Souboz. It's his son my father had planned for me to marry."

Raoul nodded. "Keller spies on me when I'm in residence on the estate. We now have proof your father's well-paid cronies *have* been watching me all these years, just as your mother told you. Her testimony means everything."

She turned away to look out at the water. "What you've learned proves that my actions in going to that interview unknowingly put you in danger."

"Not any longer."

"How can you say that?"

"The police have put both men under surveillance around the clock. I made it easy for Franz to follow me to Nice. Instead of flying, I drove the company Lexus from Paris. I made certain he saw me drive to the airport and talk to the two police officers."

"You mean he followed you?"

"In his car. One of the officers went to get your luggage. Brust followed me to the waiting helicopter. He saw me take the bag from the officer and climb aboard. The second I closed the helicopter door, both officers arrested him on the spot for stalking and took away his phone."

Fleurine wheeled around, her expression one of total disbelief. "I'm having trouble comprehending any of this."

He longed to crush her in his arms, but he couldn't. Not yet. She wasn't ready. "I know how you feel. While we were on board the helicopter, the officers texted me that Brust is in jail in Nice awaiting arraignment before the judge. This means your father won't have further contact with him. You and I are safe for the time being."

Fear darkened her violet eyes. "But Franz would have phoned him to report that you were last seen at the airport in Nice and could be anywhere. When my father can't get hold of him, I'm afraid he'll take his fury out on my family."

"No, Fleurine. First of all, he won't know what happened to Franz for a long time. More importantly, I promise that your family is being protected day and night."

"I believe you, but Raoul—when he doesn't hear from Franz, he'll call one of the cult in Switzerland to help track you down."

"We're hoping he does. Your father is the key that will give the police more names. They want to arrest all the men who murdered those monks and get confessions. Just remember, the police are surveilling him around the clock. So are my brothers who are making sure no harm comes to your mom and siblings. Everyone is on the alert."

"I'm sure you're right, but I can't stop worrying." She got up from the table and walked to the end of the terrace to look out over the sea.

He followed and put his hands on her upper arms from behind. "I realize you've been terrified for years," he murmured into her hair. "Can't you trust me for a little while longer? Your father is going to be arrested."

A tremor that he could feel shook her body.

"I've always trusted you. It's my father I can't trust. He's capable of anything. There are many things about his cruelty I learned when I had to stay with his sister. After ten years, his rage is stronger than ever."

He pulled her back against his chest. It had been so long since he'd held her in his arms. "So is my determination to stop him, Fleurine. I swear I won't let him hurt you or your family ever again. Can you let go of your fear for this next week and allow us to enjoy some time together we've never had before?"

She pulled away and turned to him. "I appreciate more than you know what you're trying to do to solve this, but we're not in school anymore, Raoul. We can't pick up where we left off. What we felt years ago has been lost. Too much of life has happened to both of us.

"I'd like to leave in the morning, and you need to get as far away from this part of the country as possible. When I get back to work, I'll think up a reason to tell my boss why I didn't stay in Nice."

Pick your battles, Raoul.

He sucked in his breath. "We'll fly to Naples in the morning and take the company jet back to Paris. I'll phone your boss and explain that the new facility for the police department didn't work out. We'll pay you and Aire-Tech for your time and a lot more."

"Thank you," she whispered, sounding shaken.

"Tell me something, Fleurine. Why were you prompted to apply for the position at Ray-onner-Tech in the first place?"

"It has a sterling reputation and offers a fantastic salary."

"I see, but there's more."

"It's true I took a chance on getting the position when I knew they wanted a person with more experience. I was hoping to be hired on probation, but fate stepped in before the interview could take place."

He frowned. "That's because I'd been called in and the receptionist told you my name. It ruined your plans. If you need money, I'll give you whatever you need, Fleurine. In fact, I have a solution so you never have to worry about that again."

"That's incredibly generous of you, but I'm able to take care of myself. Let's just be thankful no damage has been done to Ray-onner-Tech or your family's corporation. I'll go back to my job and you to yours."

Her refusal to have a heart-to-heart talk with him not only frustrated him, it crushed him. "After everything we meant to each other, is that all you have to say to me?" He didn't understand her.

"It's been so long, Raoul. Our lives have undergone tremendous changes."

"But not our memories."

"True. We'll always be able to remember wonderful times from our childhood. But we're not the same people now."

His body stiffened. Since when? "We weren't children when we kissed and talked about marriage."

"That was a teenage dream I'll always treasure. Everyone has those, but life has taken us different places. I haven't begun to achieve what I want to do."

"Like what, for example?"

"We don't have time for this, Raoul. We need to go downstairs." She started to walk out of the room. "Genevra said she and Alonzo have prepared your favorite dinner for us. I wouldn't dream of disappointing them when they love you so much and have been so kind."

Mystified and wounded by the change

in her, Raoul followed her womanly figure down the stairs. "We'll do their meal justice, but while we enjoy it, I want to know what aspirations Fleurine Dumotte has been entertaining. I used to love talking everything over with the loveliest girl on the estate. I've been waiting ten years for the privilege."

She remained curiously silent as they walked out on the lower patio overlooking the water. He helped her to the table and chairs shaded from the sun by a colorful umbrella.

Trust Genevra and Alonzo to remain invisible while the kitchen staff feted them with Neapolitan *risotto alla pescatora* and *sfogliatelle.*

Fleurine commented on everything. "I've got to get this dessert recipe from Genevra. The shape is like leaves and so unusual."

Raoul smiled at her. "They make it to resemble a monk's cowl. It came from the Santa Rosa Monastery on the Amalfi Coast in the seventeenth century. I can never get enough of the ricotta filling."

"The *boulangerie* where I worked could have made a fortune off these. Maman was a great cook and would die over the taste of it as well as the entire meal. I've never eaten such fabulous food, and this red wine is perfect."

"*Aglianico* is made here in Campania," Raoul informed her.

She sipped more of it. "No wonder you love to vacation here."

One black brow lifted. "Is it possible you're looking to open your own *boulangerie* one day?"

"Maybe after I become CEO of my own software corporation."

"I take it Paris has won your heart."

"As you know better than anyone, the proverbial City of Lights is a great place to do business and network. The cost of real estate isn't bad either."

He put down his wineglass, attempting to deal with this ambitious side of Fleurine he didn't recognize. "I'm going to ask you again. What's the real reason you applied for the position at Rayonner-Tech?"

She sat back in her chair with a sigh. "The fact that the Causcelle Corporation wants to buy it should answer your question."

With that admission he had his answer for what had been driving her. She wanted to be on top. But her shrewd response didn't sound like the Fleurine of his past. "Still, you knew they were looking for someone with more experience."

"True. I hoped they'd want me enough to give me a trial run in order to prove myself. I would have liked to be its chief engineer. But that didn't turn out when I missed my second interview. However, since flying here on the helicopter with you, I've been inspired to create my own software company even sooner than I'd planned. That form of transportation surpasses everything else, but it takes assets to afford one."

He couldn't credit that this was *his* Fleurine talking. "I don't doubt that you'll do it, but don't you have other aspirations too?"

"Like what?"

His emotions raw, Raoul pushed himself away from the table. "Like the fact that it's not too late for us to get married and have children. Remember what we talked about in the barn? I want you to be my wife so I can take care of you and love you. I promise you'll never have to worry about anything again."

She eyed him for a moment. "What you want isn't real, only a dream from long ago, Raoul. Admit we're not in love. In truth, we're strangers at this point, and you know it. I realize you see me as poor Cinderella, the Dumotte girl who was forced to wear outdated clothes and needs a prince to rescue me. But I'm not that girl, Raoul. I never was, and I would rather be in charge of my own life."

"I would never try to be in charge of your life, Fleurine."

"I'm sure you believe that, but it's a male instinct. My mother didn't find out until after her marriage." Fleurine had to keep telling him that lie. The truth was, she'd love him forever, but he deserved a woman who was his equal. She was just the Dumotte girl from the estate.

Raoul groaned inwardly. The damage Garber had done to their family had gone soul deep, robbing Fleurine of her dreams.

Had she truly grown into someone so different? This wasn't the woman he'd loved. If she were speaking honestly from her heart, then he could see that a future for the two of them would never happen. But there remained a problem. He needed her cooperation to get Dumotte arrested.

Be careful, Causcelle.

"Do you still consider me a friend, Fleurine?"

She gave him an impish smile. "As long as you promise never to waylay me again, even with the best of intentions. Still, how can I sit here and complain in these glorious surroundings?"

"They're even more glorious from the water." Raoul got up and walked over to the railing. "Alonzo's cruiser is calling to me from here. Would you take a ride with me before dark? Don't worry. I've heard what you've said, and I won't bring up marriage or our past relationship again. However, we do have to talk about your father. He's been a pall on the estate since he first arrived years ago and must pay for what he's done."

"It should have happened years ago."

"It can happen now, Fleurine. Let's go."

He went around to help her with her chair, and they headed down the side steps to the private cove below. The sun had just fallen below the horizon. Alonzo's cruiser was tied to the dock. The set up made it easy for them to step onboard. Raoul reached for a life jacket for her to wear and handed it to her, knowing she wouldn't want help putting it on.

"Thank you. I've never been on a boat like this." She didn't look at him. "Today has been a succession of firsts."

Raoul couldn't begin to describe what had happened to him today. This was an unknown Fleurine. "If you'll sit right here, I'll untie the ropes and we'll take a short spin."

He led her to a seat next to the captain's chair. In another minute he'd untied both ropes and climbed behind the wheel to start the engine. Slowly he eased them out toward a buoy. "Twilight is the perfect time to see the charm of Ischia."

After a long silence she said, "The lights from the villas and boats make me feel like I'm in fairyland. If you had to go to such lengths to get me away from Paris for this talk, you certainly couldn't have brought me to a more magical place."

His hands tightened on the wheel before he took them on a roundabout tour. When he imagined she'd seen enough, he turned off the engine so they could drift.

"I'll get right to the point," he said, turning to her. "Over the last three weeks I've been working with a criminal attorney and other authorities to build a case against your father.

To make it work, they need the testimony of three witnesses that include you, me and—"

"My mother," she supplied. "I haven't seen or talked to her since the night my father drove me to Switzerland. She doesn't know if I'm dead or alive. Even if she were willing to come forward, a spouse can't testify against her husband."

"There are exceptions," he interrupted her. "One is when the spouse has threatened a crime against the other spouse's child. Your father threatened to kill both of us at gunpoint. The other exception involves communication about a crime that took place long before the marriage of the two spouses."

She shook her head. "I don't know if she'd be willing to volunteer what she overheard, even after everything he's done. Her fear might be too great."

Raoul breathed deeply. "Once she finds out you're alive, I believe she'll do whatever it takes to free all of us and your siblings from his tyranny. I can arrange for the two of you to be together in a safe place. She'll be overjoyed to know she was able to keep you alive and safe all these years. You're the only one who can convince her that all the problems with your father will be over once she goes to the police with what she knows. They'll guarantee her safety."

He watched her clutch her hands together. "I don't see how you can guarantee anything where my father's concerned."

"You told me you trust me. Do you honestly think I would put you and your mother in jeopardy if I couldn't promise you the right outcome?"

Her head lowered. "No." He could hear her mind working. "What's your plan?"

Dieu merci. She wasn't fighting him on this. Her question filled him with unmitigated relief. "It has all been worked out with the chief detective on the case. Since you already packed for a week's vacation, we'll fly from Naples to La Racineuse in the morning."

She turned away from him.

"After we land, I'll be the only one leaving the Causcelle jet so that Keller will follow me to my work. Later, you'll leave the jet with an undercover detective who will check you in to the Petite Bergère hotel. Other undercover officers will be stationed there 24-7 to keep you safe. Another one will bring your mother to the hotel for this reunion. Your two siblings will both be working in the *fromagerie.*"

Her head came up. "That's where they are now?"

"They've been working there since high school graduation. Your father keeps them close."

"But he'll—"

"His phones are monitored around the clock, and he'll be at the dairy under the strictest surveillance. Since I will have returned to the estate, he won't have a reason to call in another cult guy yet. He'll be waiting to hear from Brust, who was arrested in Nice. This will be the perfect time to get your mother's testimony. Your father won't have any idea what's going on."

Realizing Fleurine had a lot to process, he started the engine and headed back to the Romanos' private dock in the small cove. The return didn't take long. He tied up the boat and helped her off, and together they walked along the path leading to the stone steps. When they reached the upper level of the villa, he paused outside her room before going downstairs to his.

"Think about everything tonight, and give

me your answer in the morning. I'll see you on the lower patio at eight. If the answer is no, we'll fly from Naples to Paris." The next few words were necessary, but it took all the strength he had to say them. "You have my word I'll never ask you to marry me again. *Bonne nuit,* Fleurine."

Raoul had spoken the truth about leaving her alone: Fleurine had felt it. She ran through the room to the terrace where she clung to the railing. She'd really done it now, but it had torn out her heart.

A light breeze ruffled her hair. She had no doubt Raoul would try to make it all work where her father was concerned. But it would take her being as brave as she'd been in her office when she'd thought her father might come bursting through the door and shoot her. She'd made herself a target while Paul had been pasted against the wall.

Flying to the estate with Raoul meant she needed to find the courage to be her father's target again. Not just for herself and family but for Raoul. He'd had the burden of keeping quiet about her father. All these years he'd been forced to deal with him since he ran the dairy. Because of his terrorizing hatred against the Causcelles and Catholics, Raoul's brothers hadn't even dared marry in the cathedral.

She got ready for bed but slept poorly. Deep down she suffered for Raoul, who'd been held hostage by her father. It hadn't been fair to Raoul whose one sin in life was to have been born a Causcelle. In truth only she and her mother could deal with the man who'd ruined all their lives.

To see her mother again after all these years...

By the time morning came, she had determined to do everything possible to help Raoul. Once her father was arrested, everyone could move on with their lives. As for her own, it meant loving Raoul in silence forever.

After dressing in the same apricot suit she'd worn from Paris, she joined Raoul on the patio with her suitcase. He stood there dressed in a light gray suit and white shirt, the essence of masculine perfection.

There was no man in the world like him. His fiery black eyes played over her as she walked toward him. "*Bonjour*, Fleurine."

"*Bonjour*, Raoul. I thought the Romanos

would be out here. I wanted to thank them for everything."

He shook his dark head. "I told them we were leaving early and explained we'd eat breakfast on the plane. The question is, in what direction will we head?"

The Raoul of those teenage years had vanished. Pain seared her to realize she'd done the damage that had changed their relationship. But the irony of that thought lay in the fact that they hadn't been in a relationship as adults and were virtual strangers at this point. She wasn't even going to be allowed to say goodbye to Genevra who'd told her private things about Raoul and his parents which she'd always cherish.

She lifted her head. "For everyone's sake I want my father's reign of terror to end, so I'm anxious to go along with your plan."

"*Merci*," he muttered in his deep voice. "You won't regret it. The helicopter is waiting to take us to Naples International Airport. We'll fly to La Racineuse from there." He reached for her suitcase. They walked up the side steps and around the back of the villa where the helicopter awaited them.

He opened the door and helped her inside.

The pilot smiled at her. "We meet again, Mademoiselle Millet."

"*Bonjour*, Yves."

She took a seat and strapped herself in. Raoul talked to Yves for a moment then found a seat across from her. Within seconds the rotors started, then came liftoff.

Fleurine looked out the window where she saw the Romano couple waving to them from the terrace. Tears filled her eyes as she waved back. Soon she'd find a way to thank them for being so wonderful to her.

The landscape became a blur during the short flight to the airport. Raoul didn't speak until they landed near the Causcelle jet waiting on the tarmac. "As I told you, there'll be an undercover detective on board. His name is Dennis Landrie. He'll arrange everything. I know both you and your *maman* will like him. He's following orders from the head detective in Paris. You'll be in good hands with him. Shall we go?"

She did his bidding as he helped her out of the helicopter. While they walked, he carried her suitcase. The steward welcomed her onboard the jet. When they reached the lounge compartment, a fortyish, attractive man with light brown hair stood there waiting. He wore jeans and a shirt.

"You have to be Mademoiselle Dumotte. I know Raoul has told you I'll be assisting you and your mother. I'm Dennis. It's a pleasure to meet you."

His smile made her less nervous. "You're a brave man to do this, Dennis."

"Between my boss and Raoul, we've been working out a strategy I'm confident will succeed. After we reach cruising speed, I'll discuss the plan with you."

Raoul took her arm. "Sit over here, Fleurine."

Once all three were ensconced, the seatbelt light flashed on. After she fastened hers, they taxied out to the runway. Soon they were winging their way to eastern France.

Home.

She had a hard time believing this was even happening.

The steward served them breakfast. She only ate a roll and drank some coffee. After their trays were cleared away, Dennis turned to her. "Mademoiselle Dumotte?"

"Please call me Fleur."

"*Très bien*, Fleur. When we land at Chalon

Champforgeuil, we'll stay on the jet until Raoul leaves. Then you and I will drive in a taxi the fifteen miles to the Petite Bergère hotel in La Racineuse. We'll get you settled in the room for your meeting. I understand you haven't seen your mother in ten years. That will be quite a reunion."

"It's been too long since I've seen her."

"Understood. Another undercover officer will bring your mother to the hotel."

Raoul leaned forward. "After you and Simone have talked, I'll join you, and we'll go from there. This is going to work, Fleurine."

She sucked in her breath. "I can only pray that it does. Your courage is awesome."

While he and Dennis talked, she looked out the window, getting more and more excited at the thought of seeing her dear mother again. But she'd hardly slept the night before and drifted off until it was time to land at the airport. She fastened her seat belt, but as the ground came up to meet them, she got that knot of fear in her stomach.

No matter what Raoul had said, her father would be wondering why he hadn't heard from Brust and would find some way to learn what had gone wrong in Nice.

The second the jet came to a stop, Raoul got to his feet. His dark eyes found hers. "I'll see you later at the hotel. Don't worry. We have this all covered."

She watched him leave the lounge and felt an ache in her heart for all he'd had to endure because of her father. This plan had to work!

Ten minutes later she followed Dennis out of the jet to a waiting taxi. He put her suitcase on the back seat, and they drove to the town Fleurine hadn't seen since she'd been taken away. There were a few changes, but nothing of significance. This was still home. Paris seemed as far away to her as another universe.

At ten after one they pulled up in front of the hotel. Dennis helped her out. Carrying her suitcase, he accompanied her past the front desk to a room on the second floor down the hall from the elevator. Using a key, he let them in. There were two double beds and an en suite bathroom. A basket of fruit sat on a table near a small fridge.

"Make yourself at home, Fleur. It's for you and your mother to use for as long as necessary. Officer Thibault is bringing her now.

Consider it your room until you go back to Paris."

Go back to Paris...

Fleurine freshened up in the bathroom. Her heart pounded so hard she thought she'd be sick. When she emerged, he said, "They're on their way."

"How much does my mother know?"

"Only that you've been found and that she's meeting you under the safest of circumstances to solve the problem with your father."

She couldn't sit and instead looked out the window, but it faced the rear of the hotel. "I'm frightened."

"Raoul explained to me that you've been living in fear for ten years. Let's hope today marks the beginning of a life of freedom for all of you."

Fleurine couldn't imagine a life where her father didn't dominate every facet of it. Suddenly there was a knock on the door. She jumped and whirled around in time to see Dennis open it. Her eyes caught sight of her lovely mother who was an inch shorter than Fleurine. She'd grown older, but nothing else had changed. Her light brown hair still hung down her back, and she still wore a dated white dress with long sleeves.

"Maman—" Fleurine's cry reverberated in the room before they flew into each other's arms, clinging for dear life. She could smell the wonderful scent of lavender from the soap her mother had always used.

"Ma belle fille." Tears gushed from their eyes while they rocked back and forth, never letting go. "Thank heaven you're still safe after all this time—and so beautiful!"

"So are you. How are Marti and Emma?"

"They're fine."

"Do they know anything?"

"Nothing."

"Not even about Raoul and my feelings for him years ago?"

"I knew how you felt about him, but his name has never passed my lips in all these years. It had to remain a secret to keep us all safe." Her mom's gray eyes kept staring at her. "I can't believe we're together again. It's a miracle."

"That's because of you, Maman. You saved my life when you gave me the money and birth certificate so I could escape. There's so much we need to catch up on... I don't know where to begin."

Her mother nodded. "I understand we have Raoul to thank for this reunion."

"Yes. It's a long story, and one day I'll tell you everything. What's important is that we owe you and him our lives for staying quiet about Father's criminal activities over a lifetime. Right now, let me introduce you to Detective Dennis Landrie. He's working with the head detective in Paris on this case."

He shook her mother's hand. "Madame Dumotte, you're a remarkably brave woman to come here under these circumstances. Monsieur Causcelle will be here any second while I take your testimony. I'm aware you want to be home when your son and daughter return from the *fromagerie*, so we'll get started now. I'll be recording our conversation."

Fleurine wrapped her arm around her mother's shoulders, and they walked over to the couch to sit. The detective sat on a chair opposite them and began speaking into the recorder.

"I'm taking the testimony of Simone Binoche Dumotte, fifty-nine, of La Racineuse, France. Born in said town, married at age twenty-seven to Garber Dumotte in said town. Her home is on the Causcelle estate. She's the mother of two daughters, Fleur, twenty-eight, Emma, twenty-four, and one son Marti, twenty-two, all born in said town."

While he gave background information on her mother, a knock sounded, and Raoul walked in. Nothing ever prepared her for the sight of his handsome, virile presence and dark coloring. The sight of the most attractive man on the planet caused her to gasp quietly. The man she'd pushed away.

Dennis got to his feet. "Come and join us, Raoul. We're ready to hear Madame Dumotte's story."

Raoul smiled at Fleurine's mother. "We've never been able to talk before. I've been waiting for this day for a long time, Simone. I swear you are safe here, and so are Marti and Emma."

"Thank you, Monsieur Causcelle."

"The name is Raoul. It has taken ten years for us to be our real selves."

Her eyes filled with tears. "Yes, Raoul. God bless you for what you're doing."

One black brow lifted. "Even if it means your husband will be going to prison?"

"Now that I have my Fleur back, it's a relief to tell my story at last."

Raoul had predicted her mother would cooperate once they were united. He sat down on another chair. His glance flitted to Fleurine, then he concentrated on her mother. "Please go ahead."

For the next half hour Fleurine listened to the ghastly story of the fire. As a sixteen-year-old, her mother had been in the hen house gathering eggs early in the morning when Garber and his friends suddenly came in. She had been behind a stack of empty crates and overheard everything they'd done at the church during the night. Her horror over the fire with the monks inside caused her to moan.

Garber picked up on the sound. He caught her and vowed to kill her and her family if she ever breathed a word. She'd been his hostage from that morning on. Years later he forced her to marry him under threat of death. During her testimony to Dennis, she gave him the names of the teens involved.

He praised her for her courage, then it was Fleurine's turn to give her account of what had happened in the hay barn. She and Raoul had been confronted by her father, who'd aimed his rifle at them, threatening death. After Raoul corroborated her testimony, the detective made a phone call, then stood up with a satisfied expression.

"Thanks to all of you, I now have the evidence we've needed to bring this case to a close. As we speak, Garber Dumotte is being arrested at the dairy along with Ernst Keller and the other men involved for their heinous crime committed years ago."

"But what about the men in Switzerland?" Simone had voiced the question paramount in Fleurine's mind too. She couldn't bear the thought of any of them still running loose.

Dennis smiled. "They're being arrested at this very moment. Thank you for your courage in coming forward, Madame Dumotte. A huge wrong against you and your children, against Raoul and his family, against humanity and against the Catholic Church has been righted at last."

Fleurine gripped her mother's hand as the detective walked out of the room. She lifted her eyes to Raoul. "So we're really free?" she cried.

"Like you've never been before," he answered in his deep, vibrant voice. "All it took was for the three of us to give testimony. The law is doing the rest. It's only the beginning, of course. In time your father and his friends will be tried before a jury and convicted. But what matters is that your lives are no longer held hostage by him or his henchmen. You can go anywhere, anytime, without fear."

"This is like a dream I never thought could happen," her mother murmured.

"Believe me, I know the feeling." He got to his full height. "If you're ready, I'll drive you to your house. Another officer has already taken Marti and Emma home from the *fromagerie*. They're waiting for you. I have no doubt it will be a reunion the four of you have anticipated for years."

Her mother walked over to him. "After what you've done for us, I owe you a debt of gratitude I can never repay, Raoul Causcelle."

"If you're talking gratitude, it works both ways, Simone. The Causcelle family intends to help make up for your years of suffering. I'll tell you about it when we get you home. My car is out in front." He reached for Fleurine's suitcase and headed for the hall.

Fleurine was in a daze as she caught hold

of her mother's arm. They followed him out of the hotel to a waiting black Mercedes. He helped them get in and drove them to the estate.

She stared at the back of Raoul's head with its black, luxuriant hair. He'd risked everything for this day to happen. The moment felt surreal. There was no more fear from her father. Fleurine had never known this kind of freedom before.

Yet relief from the paralyzing dread of his evil didn't mask her churning emotions where Raoul was concerned. But there was no time to examine what was going on inside her because they'd pulled up to the one-story farmhouse where she'd been born and raised. All looked familiar except for the police car out in front.

Raoul helped them from his car and carried her suitcase to the front porch. Before they reached the door, Emma flew out of the house and ran to embrace Fleurine with cries of joy. Over the years Marti had grown as tall as Raoul. They hugged long and hard.

CHAPTER FIVE

THE UNDERCOVER OFFICER who'd brought them home walked out to talk to Raoul. "My job here is finished. I'll leave them in your hands."

"Thank you for everything you've done. This is a day to go down in history."

"You can say that again. My folks had a relative who died in that fire years ago."

"Like so many others, our family had one too. Now it's over."

The two men shook hands before he walked to the police car. By now the family had gone inside. Raoul waited until Simone signaled him from the doorway to join them.

He'd never stepped on Dumotte property, let alone stepped over the threshold. Once inside, the austerity of the interior twisted his gut. But that would change now that Simone had free rein of everything, including their bank account and possessions. Raoul would make sure of it.

"Raoul? Come in the living room and explain to everyone how you managed for all of this to happen."

Fleurine sat on the couch between her siblings. Raoul sat in one of the wooden chairs opposite them next to Simone.

"After ten years, your sister and I met by accident in Paris a little over three weeks ago. She'll tell you the details in her own time. But what you need to know is that with her and Simone's help, I learned your father had hired his friends to keep me and my brothers under surveillance all these years. He hated my father and our family. If he had caught me or my family talking with anyone in your family, he would have had everyone killed."

Emma gasped. So did Fleurine who realized Raoul was still keeping quiet about his relationship with her.

"However, the accidental meeting in Paris with your sister has changed the course of all our lives. I called in the police, and they devised a plan to arrest your father for a crime against the Church. He's now in custody for that crime in La Racineuse, along with his cohorts. They'll be flown to Paris tomorrow to face trial, conviction and imprisonment."

Marti sat forward with a solemn expression. "Are you talking about the fire that burned those monks alive?"

Raoul cleared the blockage in his throat. "Yes."

"So our father *was* responsible."

"He and his friends. I realize this can't be easy for you to hear. But as Father Didier at the cathedral told me weeks ago, Garber was once an innocent child. Through being abused, he learned to hate, and God will deal with him. What's important is that he and Simone produced three wonderful children, and you have your whole lives ahead of you. That's what I want to talk to you about.

"Your father did run the dairy faithfully for years. Despite her constant fear of all of you being killed because of his threats, your mother supported him while raising you to keep you safe. Out of respect for your mom and you, our family held a meeting and want to do something for you in return.

"Emma and Marti, you can go on working at the *fromagerie* or whatever you'd like to do on the estate. But maybe you'd like to look for work elsewhere or go to college here in France. That decision is up to you. Just know the family will be funding those expenses and give you each a car of your choice. It's the least we can do."

Marti jumped to his feet. His gray-blue eyes lit up. "You really mean that?"

Simone nodded. "He means it, *mon fils*. His word is his bond."

Raoul smiled at her. "Your *maman* is a saint, Marti. The reward money offered years ago by the community for finding the person causing the fire is hers. As for the Causcelle family, we will always look after your family's needs. That includes a new car for her too. It and your truck will be out in front in the morning, Simone."

He noticed Emma sobbing against Fleurine's shoulder.

"You need to know your *maman* kept secrets all your lives, and they kept you safe. In truth, she helped your sister escape to Paris where she's been living and working all these years."

"You've been in Paris?" Emma cried. Both she and Marti stared at Simone and Fleurine in wonder.

Raoul smiled. "Did you know your mother made bakery items that she secretly sold on the estate? She's a saint. That money helped your sister when the time came to run away from your aunt in Switzerland. Your sister is a heroine too. She worked in a bakery in Paris using your mother's delicious recipes. That's how she paid for college and is now the head software engineer at Aire-Tech."

Marti looked stunned. "You're a software engineer?"

Raoul nodded. "She's a whiz. Top of her class. All of you Dumottes are exemplary people who've had to endure pain no one else can comprehend. Please keep in mind that if you don't want any help at the moment, money will be put in your individual accounts at the bank of your choice to be used however you please.

"I have one more thing to say before I have to leave. You've been given time off from the *fromagerie* to enjoy this reunion. Since the company jet will be flying your sister back to her job in Paris within five days, you're all welcome to fly with her. If you decide to come, I'll accompany you and install you in the guest suite at the *palais* where I live when I'm in Paris. It can sleep four.

"You're welcome to stay there as long as you want and enjoy the sights. Whatever your plans, the jet will be available to take you. Now I'll say good-night."

Simone followed him out to the porch. "Please, won't you stay for dinner?"

"That's very kind, but I have to get over to the dairy."

She nodded. "Words can't express my feelings, Raoul."

"I think we both have the same problem. With your willingness to have revealed the truth, our lives are forever changed. We can all relax and enjoy the future, wherever it leads."

"I'll always be in your debt for making this happen."

"It took Fleurine's courage too," he said before he realized he'd revealed the nickname for the woman he'd loved and lost.

Pushing thoughts of her from his mind, Raoul raced out to the car. He drove straight to the dairy where six police cars, two paddy wagons and an ambulance had assembled. After he got out of the car, Dennis walked over to him. "The suspects are loaded, Raoul."

"How did it go?"

"Like clockwork. Dumotte never saw it coming."

A deep sigh escaped Raoul's lips. "The Ministry of the Interior will be giving you the Medaille d'Honneur de la Police Nationale for this, Dennis. It's a privilege to have worked with you."

"This crime might never have been solved without your help."

"Simone Dumotte is the one we have to thank, Dennis. She's one saintly woman." Her sacrifice so Fleurine could escape her father's tyranny had to be her crowning glory. This arrest went a long way to help Raoul get rid of some of his guilt. He was a Causcelle and that fact had put her in danger in the first place.

"I couldn't agree more."

He eyed the ambulance. "Was someone hurt?"

"No. We brought it as a precaution."

"What's next, Dennis?"

"We'll take Dumotte, Keller, Hartzel and Richter to the jail in La Racineuse. Tomorrow they'll be transported to the airport and flown to Paris for their arraignment. The four in Switzerland will also be flown to Paris. We have it all sewn up now."

"Dieu merci." Raoul took a deep breath, trying to comprehend that the nightmare was over. "What else can I do to help?"

"Nothing for the time being. I'll stay in touch with you."

"Then, I'll go into the dairy to explain everything to the workers. A new head has to be named tonight."

"Life goes on, doesn't it?"

"Amen." Raoul patted the man's shoulder and had just started walking toward the entrance when his brothers came rushing toward him. All three of them teared up as they hugged.

What would Raoul have done without them guarding the Dumotte family? They'd helped him with everything.

"This marks the beginning of a new era," Nic spoke in a broken voice.

Jean-Louis let out a long sigh. "Thank heaven Dumotte is gone with all his evil cronies."

"We'll tell Papa the truth tonight," Raoul announced. "He loved Gregoire, and this news will make a new man of him. First, however, we need to go in and announce that Gaston will be the new head of the dairy. He should have been put in charge years ago."

The second they entered the building, all the workers stood in the aisle shouting *Bravo!* and clapping hard. Each one came up to shake their hands and thank them for getting rid of Garber, whom they'd secretly named the *menace de Saône*.

Dumotte's crime had not only put the Saône department in eastern France on the map, everyone had suffered because of it.

And no one more than Simone and her children.

Raoul didn't dare dwell on the reunion going on in their home. The thrilling period of his teenage life with Fleurine had come to an official end.

He no longer recognized the girl he'd loved. A beautiful, determined and talented woman had taken her place. Someone, it seemed, who could not love him. He had no choice but to let her go.

After sending Dumotte to prison at last, he realized a miracle had happened. Maybe one more lay in store for him. The next time Raoul met with Pascal in Paris, he'd go to his cousin's home for dinner and meet the woman who might be the perfect match for him.

Another thunderous cry of approval broke out when Raoul announced that Gaston Farouche had been named the new head of the Causcelle dairy. While everyone celebrated the welcome news, Raoul and his brothers left to drive to the chateau.

They found their *papa* in the family room, putting a puzzle together with Françoise's great aunt after dinner. Françoise sat nearby reading a book. Jean-Louis gave his wife a kiss and asked her to wheel Nadine to her room. He and his brothers needed time alone with their father.

Louis looked up. "Well, well. You're back, Raoul. What's going on with the triumvirate tonight?"

They took a seat. "We have vital news."

His chin lifted. "That sounds serious."

"It *is*, Papa," Jean-Louis murmured, "but in a way that should bring peace to your soul as well as to the estate and the Church."

"My soul has been at peace for years."

"Except for one thing," Nic interjected.

Their father looked away. "*Eh bien, mes fils*. Don't keep me in suspense."

Raoul leaned forward. "The men responsible for the monastery fire that killed Gregoire and the monks have been arrested. Soon they will face imprisonment."

Louis's bald head turned toward Raoul in amazement. "Who did it?"

"Brace yourself, Papa. Garber Dumotte, Keller, Hartzel and Richter, along with four others rounded up in Switzerland."

Their father shook his head. "Garber?" he whispered.

"His wife Simone gave testimony to the police. She knew what he did and held her peace under threat of death all these years. She also helped Fleur escape after he threatened her and me. It turns out Garber wanted to marry Maman. Maybe you knew that."

"I suspected."

"When she chose you, he couldn't handle it and wanted to hurt both of you in a way to make you suffer."

His father moaned. "He accomplished his purpose and hurt you too."

"But that's old history now, and Gaston Farouche has been named the new head of the dairy."

"Excellent choice." After a long pause he said, "All this happened today?"

"That's right, and the world is a better place for it."

Tears dripped down his cheeks. "Poor Simone and her children."

"They're going to be fine."

He stared at the three of them. "*Mes fils*, we need to help that family."

No one had a bigger heart than their father. "It's being done," Raoul assured him. "More importantly, we hope this news will help you sleep better from now on."

Fleurine loved it that their mother was in charge for the first time. They'd just finished dinner. The last few days with the family had been a healing time for all of them. They'd strengthened their bonds and found joy being together.

"Emma? Marti? Have you two decided what you'd like to do? Raoul has texted that he'll come by here at eight in the morning to take Fleur to the airport."

There'd been no text to Fleurine, no greeting, no conversation or questions. He'd kept his promise and hadn't come near since leaving her and her mother at the door of their house four days ago. It shouldn't have surprised her. He'd always been a man of his word, but it brought her indescribable pain.

Marti eyed their mother. "We've never been anywhere, so I'd like to go to Paris and stay in that *palais* for a few days. I don't know about work or school yet."

Emma nodded. "I'd like to do the same thing. What about you, Maman? Will you come with us?"

Nothing had been settled where her siblings' future plans were concerned. The thought of leaving her mother for long periods of time tormented Fleurine.

"I don't think so. While you're gone, I'd like to do some shopping and visit my friends."

Marti grinned. "In your new Renault."

"No one deserves free time more than you, *chère* Maman," Fleurine commented. She looked at her siblings. "I'm thrilled you guys are coming with me. After my work we'll go out for dinner to some famous places, and I'll show you around. We'll shop for new clothes, get new hairdos. The works!"

"I can't wait!" Emma cried.

"Then, I think we'd better do the dishes

and get our packing done. Eight comes early. We'll eat breakfast on the jet."

Marti let out a whoop of excitement before helping to clear the table.

Later that night as Fleurine was on her way to bed, her mother stopped her in the hallway. "I've loved our time together." She hugged her.

"I'll visit whenever I can and phone you every day, Maman. If you want to move to Paris, you can live with me. Just say the word."

"No. My home is here, but I'll visit." She smiled at her. "Before I go to bed, come in my room and talk to me for a minute." They went inside. "I'm curious about something. When did Raoul start calling you Fleurine?"

Her heart thudded. *What?*

"We were on the porch when he accidentally called you that on the day he dropped you off here at the house."

Fleurine swallowed hard. "He nicknamed me that after I turned seventeen."

Her mother smiled. "It's beautiful and suits you perfectly. You never said a word to me, but it's obvious you captured this young man's heart before your father tore you from our family." Her eyes misted over. "I'm so sorry. Garber said he caught you in the barn with Raoul."

"Yes. I went there to say goodbye to him, but that was a long time ago."

"And now you're living a full life in Paris?"

"I am, and I love it."

"Is there a man you're interested in?"

"I've dated from time to time, but no one special."

"Please tell me how you actually happened to meet up with Raoul again."

"There are so many things to tell you. You have to know the beginning first. Within a month of arriving in Paris I had my name legally changed to Laure Millet so I couldn't be traced."

"You smart girl."

"Now leap ahead to a few months ago where I was working as a software engineer at Aire-Tech. Another engineer working there named Paul began pursuing me. We had one date, and that was it. I wasn't interested, but he became impossible, so I decided to try for employment elsewhere. I decided to go for an interview with Rayonner-Tech, the best software company in Paris. That turned out to be a move that has changed my life.

"As the receptionist led me to the conference room for my second interview, she mentioned that Raoul Causcelle was in there with the CEO."

"Oh, *ma chère Fleur*. What a shock!"

"You have no idea. It frightened me so badly I tripped and hurried out of the building. Later, Raoul came to my office at Aire-Tech to find out what had happened to Mademoiselle Millet. He'd been called to sit in on the interview. Causcelle planned to buy Rayonner-Tech but needed to approve the person who'd be hired for the chief engineer position."

"Meaning *you*. That's incredible. I bet you had no trouble recognizing him."

She hugged her arms to her waist. "No. He's a breed apart from other men."

"Your transformation must have shocked him."

"You mean no more Cinderella-in-white."

Her mother studied her for a moment. "Then what happened?"

"We met again at the *palais* where he stays when in Paris. I told him I'd never married."

A slow smile broke out on her mother's dear face. "When he learned you were still single, it's obvious he wasted no time arranging for your father's arrest. What else haven't you told me?"

Fleurine knew what her mother was getting at. "He arranged a bogus interview for me three weeks later in Nice where he showed up. We flew to Ischia, Italy, and stayed with friends of his family overnight. He wanted us to pick up where we'd left off, but I took your advice because you've never led me wrong."

"What are you talking about?"

"You sent me a note with that money ten years ago. It said, *You and Raoul were born into separate worlds. You were never meant to step out of them to be together. Remember that a woman can be fulfilled and successful without a man.*"

"I said that because you were only seventeen."

"Even so, being with him again made me realize you'd spoken the truth. We come from separate worlds. He's a bachelor with a lifestyle most men would give anything to have. I've taken your advice to heart and am determined to own my own software company someday. I haven't looked back, and it's because of you. You're a saint, Maman, and I adore you. Now we both need to get to bed."

She kissed her cheek and rushed out in the hall to the bedroom she was sharing with Emma.

"I'm so excited, Fleur. I've never been on any kind of plane before."

Fleurine laughed. "I know how you feel. You'll love it."

"Do you have to go to work tomorrow?"

"Of course not. I'll call my boss and ask for a few more days off. He'll understand when he learns you and Marti have come with me for a short visit."

They talked until they turned out the lights. Emma kept her distracted from the conversation she'd had with her mother until her sister fell asleep. Unfortunately, she tossed and turned for the rest of the night. She kept remembering the worried look in her mother's eyes after she'd hurried out of the bedroom. What had caused it?

Worse, her dreams were filled with Raoul and that moment in Ischia when he'd asked her again to marry him. She'd turned him down and wanted to die.

Long before it was time to get up, Fleurine showered and dressed once more in her apricot suit she liked for travel. She put out one of her skirts and print blouses she'd brought so Emma could wear them. Her sister was the same height, so she also let her borrow a pair of her flats.

"Oh, Fleur—these clothes look like my friends' outfits! I can't believe it." She ran around the house showing Marti and their mother. "I need to get my hair cut. So do you, Marti. Yours is too long."

"That's one of the first things I'm going to do."

"What's the other?"

"Buy some cargo pants and sandals."

Fleurine smiled as she watched the two of them step out of the eighteenth century into life. The giant hand of their father no longer crushed them in his grasp. She had Raoul to thank for their liberation. But knowing he would be coming by for them in a few minutes had made her restless.

Her mother came out to the porch where Fleurine waited with her suitcase. "I'll get rid of their clothes while they're with you in

Paris," Simone whispered. "Make sure Emma
gets a haircut like yours. It will suit her too."

Fleurine turned to her. "You're so wonderful, Maman. It's hard to leave you, but I
promise I'll be back soon."

"I have no doubt of it. Don't tell the others,
but I'm following your example. Later today
I'm interviewing for the position of head pastry chef at the Beauchamps *boulangerie* in
La Racineuse."

With a cry, Fleurine threw her arms around
her. When she let her go, Raoul had pulled
up in the Mercedes.

Her heart leaped as she watched the man
she used to think of as a dark-haired pirate get
out and walk towards them. Today he wore
a tan suit with white shirt and striped tie. In
the news or otherwise, he and his brothers always looked like they'd just stepped off the
front page of *GQ*.

"Bonjour, tout le monde!" he called out.

"Bonjour, Monsieur Causcelle!" Emma and
Marti had come out on the porch with their
overnight bags and hurried toward the car
like young children on holiday. The scene
tugged at Fleurine's heart.

He came closer. His black eyes blazed. *"Eh*

bien, Simone. It looks like everyone is ready for a trip to Paris. Are you prepared to be an empty nester for a few days?"

"I'll manage somehow," she answered with a broad smile. Fleurine knew her mother was excited to get going on a career for herself.

"You have my phone number, and I have yours. Be assured I'll return your children safely to you."

"I know you will. Bless you, Raoul."

After another hug, Fleurine hurried down the steps to the car carrying her suitcase before Raoul could take it from her.

He loaded their cases into the trunk and opened the rear door. The three of them got in the back. After he took his place behind the wheel, he honked and waved to their mother before pulling away. They drove through the estate past the chateau in the distance and reached the highway leading to the airport in Chalon Champforgeuil.

She experienced another surreal moment riding in Raoul's car with her excited siblings on either side of her. They talked about what they wanted to do on their trip, while Raoul made several calls on his phone. During his last one, he caught her staring at him through the rearview mirror.

Feeling uneasy, she turned her head to look out the window. Fleurine had let him know there could be nothing between them. Her father had been arrested. That action ended any more association with Raoul. But it was difficult not to look at him while they were together in the car.

After her dreams of last night, she knew she'd thrown away the possibility of something wonderful by turning him down. She'd have to be careful and stay occupied with her siblings after they boarded the jet. Once in Paris, she and Raoul would go their separate ways for good.

"Wow," Marti blurted when they reached the airfield and parked near the Causcelle jet. Several airport workers came running and helped with their luggage.

"*Eh bien*, you two." Raoul smiled at her siblings. "Let's get onboard. Once we're seated, we'll buckle up and be off. It's a perfect fall day, so I know you'll enjoy your first flight."

They followed him up the steps and into the lounge compartment. Fleurine knew how overwhelmed they were feeling. The

Causcelle lifestyle couldn't be compared to anything they'd known before now. Raoul introduced them to the pilot and steward who promised to serve them breakfast once they were in the air. Raoul had a way…

Fleurine found her own seat while he answered their questions. He soon had them laughing and feeling totally comfortable. This was the Raoul who'd charmed her from the first second she'd met him as a young girl on the estate.

The seat-belt sign flashed on, and they all buckled up. Fleurine stared out the window so she wouldn't be caught a second time gazing at his incredibly handsome features and dark hair.

Once they'd reached cruising speed, breakfast with all the trimmings turned out to be one happy event. After the steward cleared their trays, Raoul asked them what they would like most to do after they arrived in Paris.

Marti spoke first. It came as a surprise since he'd always been quiet and rarely assertive. "You mentioned we could stay at the *palais* where you live when you come to Paris. Is it a real *palais*?"

"It used to be and looks like one from the outside. My sister's suite on the main floor is vacant with two bedrooms. You and your sister are welcome to stay in it for as long as you want." He turned to Emma. "What sounds good to you?"

"I—I'd like to stay there too," she stammered. "Is that all right with you, Fleur?"

"I would have been surprised if you'd said you wanted to stay with me." Who would choose her apartment after being offered the world?

Raoul nodded. "Then, it's settled. The *palais* has laundry service. There's also a kitchen staff that provides meals day and night. Just call on the phone. We keep an Audi in the parking lot if you want to drive around. Guy, the man in the foyer, will give you key. I'll be on the second floor in my own suite in case you need to phone me for anything."

They plied him with questions for what felt like ages. Then to her surprise he got to his feet. In the next breath he pulled two envelopes from his pocket and handed them to her siblings. "This money set up in your own accounts is for you to go on a shopping spree.

Fleur will help you navigate around Paris and find what you're looking for.

"After we arrive, we'll drive to the *palais* to get you situated. I have work today, but tonight it will be my pleasure to take all of you to dinner on top of the *Tour Eiffel*. It's a wonderful place to drink in the atmosphere of Paris on your first visit."

Emma squealed for joy. As for Marti, Fleurine thought he looked like he'd died and gone to heaven.

Following Raoul's unexpected dinner invitation, and his display of unimagined kindness and generosity, the seat-belt warning flashed. He sat down once more, and they buckled up for the descent. She needed another belt fastened around her chest to quiet her palpitating heart. The sooner she didn't ever have to see him again, the better.

CHAPTER SIX

RAOUL DROVE THEM into Paris from the airport. He alerted Guy to make sure his sister Corinne's suite would be ready for the Dumotte family. If ever three people deserved to be showered with a few gifts after a lifetime of emotional abuse, they did.

Once upon a dream he'd planned to marry Fleurine and spoil her with everything her heart could desire. But those days were over. Though he would always be in love with his memory of her, she'd changed beyond recognition. They could never have a relationship now.

Still, he found it cathartic to do something of value for Simone's younger children who deserved a fresh start. After he pulled up in front of the *palais*, he walked inside the foyer and introduced them to Guy. The man had a friendly, warm nature they would enjoy.

"Have a great day, guys," Raoul said a few minutes later. "I'll meet you out in front at seven thirty, and we'll enjoy a night out." Avoiding Fleurine's eyes, he returned to his car and took off for headquarters a block away.

"Hey, Raoul," his cousin cried out when he walked in the office. "I'm so glad to see you. My wife and I were just talking about you so we could set up a dinner engagement for tonight with you-know-who."

"Tonight I'm busy, but how about tomorrow night? A river cruise on the Seine?" He needed his cousin to divert his attention while he entertained Fleurine and her siblings one more night. Then he could walk away forever.

Pascal's head flew back. "Are you serious?"

"I'm playing host to the Dumotte family while they're in Paris."

"You *what*?"

"I know what you're thinking, but no. Fleurine and I will never be together, but Jean-Louis and I are doing this for their family. I'll tell you the reason later. Do you think you and Janelle could join us and bring this new woman with you? I'll be going back to La Racineuse the day after tomorrow, so that might be the only time for a while."

"I'll phone my wife. If it can work, I'll let you know."

"*Bien*. We'll board the cruise from the Pont de Bir-Hakeim at eight o'clock."

He left his cousin and walked down the hall to George's inner sanctum. His first priority was to call Philippe Charbon, the CEO at Aire-Tech. After he was put through, he explained he was phoning for the chief of police in Nice. The chief was a friend of his father's and was willing to help.

"The real-estate arrangement fell through so we couldn't use Mademoiselle Millet after all. She flew back to Paris this morning. We've reimbursed her and your company for your willingness to loan her to us. If we can find another property, we'll be calling both of you again. *Merci bien, Monsieur* Charbon."

With that lie taken care of, he called Marcel, the maître d'hôtel at the *Tour Eiffel* restaurant.

"Ah, Raoul!" he exclaimed excitedly. "What can I do for you?"

"Tonight I'm bringing guests for dinner, two women and a man. We'll be there by eight o'clock. They'll order whatever they want, but I'd like the best champagne served. Will you seat us at a window where they can see everything? This is their first trip to Paris."

"I understand and will find the perfect spot, Raoul. What about flowers?"

"Perhaps a red rose in a vase for both women at their places."

"A delightful touch. *Merci,* Raoul. *À bientôt.*"

Raoul hung up and made a third call to Simone. She'd left her voice mail on. He let her know they'd arrived. "All is well with your *enfants.*"

For his last call, he phoned Jules Vaugier at Rayonner-Tech. "Jules? Have you filled the position of chief software engineer yet?"

"No. We have to get the best person, and I'm not convinced we've found one yet. It was a shame that Laure Millet had that accident. The reports on her were outstanding, even if she hadn't worked in the business ten years."

"I agree, and I have good news. She had a slight ankle sprain but is now back to normal. I'm impressed with the reviews on her from all the Aire-Tech clients. My instincts tell me she'd be a good candidate for the position if you decide to hire her on probation. Who knows? The CEO at the Causcelle Corporation might still be willing to talk business with you."

"You think?"

"You never know."

"That's true. I'll get Gabrielle to contact her about another interview. I'm curious to find out what your gut is telling you."

"Best of luck, Jules."

Raoul clicked off, wanting this to be his farewell gift to Fleurine. She'd hoped to work for Rayonner-Tech. Heaven knew she deserved it with her outstanding credentials and all she'd been through.

He got up from the desk and walked back to Pascal's office. "Tell me, cousin. What is the latest decision on Rayonner-Tech?"

"We're still waiting to find out who they hired for the chief software engineer. Janelle is working on that date for tomorrow night. I'll call you when I know anything."

"Perfect. Now I've got to run."

Out in the car, he phoned Guy and learned that their guests had left in the Audi to shop. With that good news, he returned to the *palais* where he could relax in his own suite and make a ton of calls.

The first one to his father made Raoul

happy. He could tell his *papa* had definitely found peace after learning of Garber's arrest. The police had informed Father Didier about it. He paid a visit to the chateau to thank Louis and the family on behalf of the Church. Their gratitude caused his father to weep over the phone.

After ordering a sandwich from the kitchen, Raoul was able to get hold of Jean-Louis.

"What's going on, *frérot*?"

"The Dumotte family is now installed at the *palais* in Corinne's old suite."

"Does that mean Fleurine and her mother too?" Jean-Louis and Nic had always known about his love for her. But he'd let them know there was no possibility of a future for them now.

"It turns out Simone wanted to stay home. As you know, Fleurine has her own apartment and will probably go back and forth while her siblings are in Paris. It's just Emma and Marti I'm concerned about. Guy's being a great help to them."

"There's no one better."

"The reason I'm calling is that I could really use your expertise. All the work you've done for the vets is phenomenal, and I'm hoping you can help them."

"What Garber did to those poor kids was criminal. I'll do whatever I can."

"Have I told you lately how glad I am you're back from the army?"

Jean-Louis laughed. "No one is happier than I am."

Raoul knew his brother's life had turned around since his return. Françoise had become his great joy. "If your wife doesn't mind, would you be able to fly to Paris in the morning and meet with them in their suite? I'll have the jet waiting at the Chalon Champforgeuil Airport for you. They need guidance about their future education. You're the one to do it, and you know all the important contacts."

"Will do. I should be there by ten thirty."

They hung up, and he called Damond, his assistant at the estate office. They discussed business and a few problems before it was time to shower and shave for the night out.

Dressed in a navy suit and tie, Raoul left the *palais* at twenty after seven and went out to the parking area for his car. He pulled up in front of the entrance and waited.

Between becoming new hairstyles that brought out their blond hair and attractive features, he hardly recognized his guests. Emma wore a valentine-red cocktail dress. Marti looked like the elegant young man about town in a charcoal suit and paisley tie. Their shopping spree had produced stylish results. Raoul took a picture of them with his phone to send to Simone.

He'd already been stunned by Fleurine's transformation weeks ago, but he couldn't take his eyes off her in a breathtaking black sheath with long sleeves. They climbed in the back and couldn't stop talking about their adventures all the way to the Champs de Mars.

Fleurine didn't say anything. Her siblings talked nonstop, making it difficult to get a word in. Raoul couldn't remember the last time he'd been so entertained. The oohs and aahs continued when they got up close to the *Tour Eiffel*. They might be in their early twenties, but their reactions were childlike, and Raoul couldn't stop smiling.

Like his brothers, he'd always felt guilty about the Causcelle billions, but not tonight. It brought him joy to spread some happiness to Garber's innocent children. The fact that

Fleurine didn't fight him and his family on doing what they could for her mother and siblings made this what his father called a *sacred experience.*

After he parked the car, they wove their way through the ever-present crowds and rode the elevator to the restaurant. Marcel came hurrying up to them.

"Soyez la bienvenue, Raoul!" He clapped his hands.

"*Merci*, Marcel. Meet my guests Emma, Marti and Fleur Dumotte from eastern France."

"*Enchanté*. Let me show you to your table. It's ready for you."

They followed him through the room to a table next to the window that looked out over Paris.

"Please be seated, and we'll take care of you."

Raoul purposely helped Emma, leaving Marti to assist Fleurine. Soon a waiter came with menus, and orders were taken. Next came the *sommelier*, who poured the champagne.

After he walked away, Raoul raised his glass. "You guys look terrific! I want to welcome you to Paris and propose a toast.

May this be the beginning of new hopes and dreams."

They all clinked glasses and sipped his favorite vintage.

Emma beamed at him. "I feel like I'm in a dream right now. Thank you, thank you for everything you've done for us, Raoul."

Marti nodded. "All this is fantastic."

"You've done too much," Fleurine murmured, avoiding his gaze.

He expected that from her. "Not at all. There's more to come. I'll tell you about it while we eat."

They chose fish since they rarely ate it at home. Raoul loved it too. At the end of their meal, he tapped his glass with a spoon. "My father is grateful for Marti and Emma's work at the dairy and for everything your mother has done to bring your father to justice. Now he'd like to do something for you in return. Maybe you want to stay on the estate and work. Maybe not. But he's hoping you'll consider going to college here in Paris the way my brothers and I did.

"I have business tomorrow morning, but my brother will be meeting with you at the *palais*. He'll arrive around ten thirty to talk about your plans for the future. He's been helping returning veterans go to school to earn degrees or to learn a trade. Jean-Louis has many connections and can answer a lot of questions you might have. If or when you decide to fly home, I'll make sure the jet is available."

"You're unbelievable," Marti blurted with tears in his eyes.

Raoul shook his head. "My entire family admires you. It's a pleasure to bring you and your mother a little happiness. Now it's late. If you're ready to go, I'll get you back to the *palais* for a good night's sleep."

Emma gazed at him. "Would it be all right if I took this rose? I'd like to keep it to remember."

"By all means."

Fleurine said nothing before he got to his feet and walked them to the restaurant entrance. Marcel shook their hands before they went down the elevator.

In the car Emma exclaimed, "I'll never forget this night for as long as I live."

"You can say that again," Marti agreed.

Raoul started the engine, and they took off. "I, too, enjoyed it more than I can say."

Again there was no comment from Fleurine. He knew she couldn't wait to say goodnight, and this caused him unimaginable pain, but she had made her feelings clear. All he could do now was see that her family were happy. Fleurine was lost to him…

Before long they reached the *palais,* and the three of them got out of the back, but Emma held back.

"I'll be thanking you over and over again for all you've done for us and are still doing." Her eyes shone as she looked up at Raoul. "It's so strange to think we could live on the estate all these years and never have known each other. Yet now, I feel so close to you and your family. I wish I could do something personal and important for you."

He smiled at her. She had that same sweetness and vibrancy he'd seen in Fleurine during those growing-up years. It touched his heart. Her lovely gray eyes didn't have violet flecks, but in some respects she resembled her elder sister, especially with her new hairdo.

"There *is* one thing you can do for me, Emma. Don't let anything stop you from finding your happiness. *That's* what's important."

"I think I already have."

Fleurine overheard them talking. She thanked Raoul before hurrying inside to their suite for the night in order to get a grip on her emotions. Tomorrow night she'd go back to her apartment. Though she'd said goodbye to him in Ischia, minutes ago the sight of a lovesick Emma gazing up at Raoul as if he were her whole world had turned Fleurine inside out. It never occurred to her that something like this could happen.

All Raoul had to do was be kind to Emma and flash her his heart-stopping smile. Like every smitten woman within his orbit, the very last thing on earth her vulnerable sister would want was to escape. Emma was a twenty-four-year-old woman, no longer a child. She'd never met a man to compare to Raoul.

She never would...

Fleurine thought back to her conversation with Emma at the house. Her sister had admitted to having a slight crush on one of the guys working in the estate hothouse. But any chance of dating him had been impossible since their father had arranged for her dreaded marriage to a man in Switzerland at the end of the year.

Now Raoul's intervention had changed everything for Emma who couldn't stop talking about Raoul and how wonderful he was. Fleurine groaned. Emma knew nothing of Fleurine's history with Raoul. There was no question her sister had fallen for him. This called for an intervention of her own making.

Before it was too late, she would have to tell her everything. The mere thought of them being together brought such exquisite pain she could hardly breathe.

While she agonized, Marti came in. He was over the moon about everything, especially Raoul who'd won her brother's heart from the beginning.

"C'est un etalon!"

That was Marti's French slang for the American word *stud*. High praise indeed. Fleurine looked past him. "Where's Emma?"

"She's still talking to Raoul about living here at the *palais* if she decides to stay in Paris."

How well Fleurine understood what drove

her sister! Tomorrow she'd have a serious talk with her. Right now, it was time for bed.

Fleurine experienced another bad night with little sleep. Nothing had been settled where her siblings were concerned. Raoul had orchestrated everything which meant she couldn't avoid him altogether. At least not yet.

Jean-Louis arrived at the appointed time the next morning. Like Raoul, he was gorgeous and also had a way that charmed her siblings. He asked the right questions and showed an interest that made them feel incredibly comfortable.

When they'd finished eating, he looked around. "I did some snooping and discovered that the two of you graduated from high school with excellent grades. That means I can get you enrolled at a university here. After listening to you, I would advise that you attend the Sorbonne here in Paris and take the normal general classes to get started. There will be housing available. How does that sound?"

"Fantastic!" her siblings blurted in unison.

When he smiled his slow smile, it reminded Fleurine of Raoul, something she didn't need right now.

"*Très bien*. Then, let's leave now and get you two registered. Classes started two weeks ago, but I have no doubt you can catch up. Later in the day Raoul will meet us at one of our car dealerships and you can each pick out a new car you would like."

At the mention of Raoul, Fleurine's heart turned over. She got to her feet. "Before any more plans are made, we need to tell our mother what's going on and get her approval. Right?" She stared at them.

Marti pulled out his phone. "I'll call her now and put her on speaker phone." Fleurine would never forget the look of elation on her brother's face. There was no stopping him.

Their mother answered and an animated conversation ensued. Jean-Louis took over and explained what had been discussed. "It's up to you, Simone."

"You're giving my children a priceless gift. It sounds like they've made up their minds."

"We have!" Emma affirmed. "Are you okay with it?"

"What mother in her right mind wouldn't be?" She laughed.

"Guess what? We get to pick out new cars today!" This from Marti.

"I know I love my new car, *mes enfants*. Have fun. I'll see you on your first break home. Thank you, Monsieur Causcelle, from the bottom of my heart."

Another burst of excitement came out of both of them. "We'll call you tonight," Emma assured her. "Love you, Maman."

Two hours later, after leaving the student office at the Sorbonne, Jean-Louis drove them to the main Causcelle car dealership in Paris. After he'd parked, Raoul and another man walked toward them while Fleurine got out of the back seat. No matter how hard she tried, she couldn't prevent her pulse from racing when she saw him.

But it was impulsive Emma who dashed toward Raoul. "Marti and I are now enrolled at the Sorbonne because of you and your family. We're overwhelmed with gratitude." In the next instant she raised up to kiss his hard jaw with a familiarity that shocked Fleurine.

Always the gentleman, Raoul patted her shoulder and moved toward the rest of them. "Since you're now matriculated, I'd like you to meet Pierre Amant, the manager, who will help you. He's going to walk around with you, answer any questions and let you do a test drive. When you see something you like, come back over here and we'll talk."

"Let's get started," Fleurine urged them, not wanting to monopolize Raoul or his brother. "We can't afford to waste Monsieur Amant's time."

For the next hour they followed the manager around to inspect the new cars. In the end Marti chose an Alpine and talked Emma into buying one too. She loved the blue. He picked silver.

The manager took them inside the dealership to finish up business and congratulated them for their excellent choices. He told them to come back in the morning. The cars would be serviced, washed and ready to go.

They walked back out to Jean-Louis's car where the two brothers were still talking.

Raoul turned to them. "Tell you what. We'll go back to the *palais* and get ready for a dinner cruise on the Seine."

"You're kidding!" Emma cried.

"You'll love it," Jean-Louis interjected. "I'll call ahead for a reservation on *Le Capitaine Fracasse*. The food and wine are spectacular."

Raoul nodded. "Everyone should take the

cruise once because the monuments are illuminated. It's a history lesson that takes you past seventeen sites including La Cathédrale Notre-Dame, my favorite."

"At night *La Tour Eiffel* is also amazing," Jean-Louis added.

Marti nudged Emma. "Are we lucky or what?" But his sister's eyes were focused on Raoul. Emma appeared oblivious to anything else going on around her, sending an unmistakable message to Fleurine.

Her chest tightened, and she hurried to get back in the car before...

Before *what*, Fleurine? She couldn't answer that question. After returning to the *palais*, she rushed inside their suite. Marti followed.

She turned to him. "Where's Emma?"

"Still talking to Raoul about living here instead of a dorm near the university. I'm going to shower and get ready."

By the time Emma came in, Fleurine had showered and put on her dress for the evening. She would have to wait another night to go back to her apartment. "I've been waiting for you."

"It won't take me long to get dressed."

"Marti told me you were talking to Raoul

about living here at the *palais* while you attend college."

"Yes. He said it was fine with him."

Fleurine drew in a quick breath. "That may be, but it's really up to Jean-Louis, who runs the *palais*. In any event, I want you and Marti to live with me at my furnished apartment if you end up staying in Paris. My place has a guest bedroom and a sofa that is a pullout bed. You and Marti can live with me for as long as you want."

"But he already loves it here at the *palais*, and Raoul lives here. He said he'll always be willing to help us."

"Emma, there's something you don't understand. Raoul only stays here when he comes to Paris on occasion. He lives in the chateau on the estate and runs it."

A frown broke out on her face. "Why are you being negative about this?"

Whoa...

She leaned forward. "I guess you didn't understand what I told you at the house. This *palais* has been turned into a hostel for returning vets. It's Jean-Louis Causcelle's humanitarian project to help returning vets. No women live here."

"But—"

"No *but*s, Emma. Raoul and his brother are doing this favor for our family, but it's only through tomorrow. Once you pick up your cars, it's over. Look at all they have provided. We can't take any more advantage of them. Their family arranged to buy both of you a car. They opened bank accounts for you and are giving us an evening out to remember forever. Tonight has to be the end of it."

Her sister sat down on the end of one of the beds, not happy with their conversation. "Raoul is the most fabulous man I've ever met or known, Fleur. I can't begin to explain how he makes me feel. He's bigger than life and so handsome I can't think when I look at him."

Stifling another moan, Fleurine got up from the chair. "The Causcelle triplets have a reputation for making women feel that way. Just remember they come from a family of remarkable people like their father. Louis Causcelle gave our father the head dairy job all those years ago. They are decent, honorable people. As Maman says, they're in a league all their own. We need to show respect."

Emma walked over to the closet to get her

dress. "Maman said Raoul is the only one not married yet."

She struggled not to say anything. "That's right. When he does come to Paris, his evenings out with glamorous women are on the news. It's clear he's a confirmed bachelor."

One eyebrow lifted. "Maybe not for much longer."

Non, non, non.

Fleurine's stomach muscles clenched in response. "Please tell me I didn't hear you say that."

"What's wrong with you, Fleur? You're not my mother."

True. That's what she sounded like to her twenty-four-year-old sister. Fleurine headed for the door. "It's time to go. Marti is waiting for us in the living room."

CHAPTER SEVEN

"Raoul?"

Pascal's voice could be heard through the crowd of diners seated in the big dining room restaurant aboard the Capitaine Fracasse. Raoul stood up and motioned him over to their table. Janelle accompanied him along with an attractive, redheaded woman.

After he hugged his cousin and Janelle, Pascal said, "Raoul, I'd like you to meet one of my father's new assistants at the Sorbonne, Dr. Sylvie Moreau. She's an historian who's an expert in Egyptology."

"My oncle Blaise is a fortunate man," Raoul commented and shook her hand. "May I introduce you to the Dumotte family from La Racineuse. Fleur is the top software engineer at Aire-Tech. Emma and Marti will be attending the Sorbonne starting tomorrow. It will be their first college experience."

"I know what that's like," Sylvie said and smiled with a genuine warmth Raoul could feel. "If you need anything, come to the office of Dr. Causcelle in the history department, and I'll be happy to assist you in any way I can. I know you're going to love it there."

"Thank you," they murmured.

Raoul sat down at the rectangular table next to Dr. Moreau. Pascal and his wife sat on his other side. They faced Jean-Louis and the Dumotte family, and dinner was served.

While his amiable cousin and wife talked to Fleurine and her siblings, Raoul made a monumental effort to drag his attention from the woman who had captured his heart and focus it on the woman they'd thought might be perfect.

She came as a pleasant surprise. Throughout dinner they discussed her teaching schedule and the latest history books his oncle Blaise had written. Raoul found she'd led a fascinating life during her work in Egypt. When the cruise ended, he told her he would get in touch with her the next time he was in Paris.

Two limos were waiting for them when

they went ashore. "You've done me a favor, cousin. I'll be calling you soon."

"What do you know." A smiling Pascal gave him a hug. Jean-Louis left with the three of them.

Raoul followed Marti into the limo with the others. They raved about the salmon fillets with spinach mousse and asparagus. When they arrived at the *palais*, Raoul helped them out and went into the foyer with them.

"I'll say good-night to all of you here."

"Won't you come in for a little while?" Emma pleaded with him. "We want to thank you for everything."

"You already have a dozen times. Unfortunately I have to leave for the airport at six in the morning. But Jean-Louis will be by at seven to drive you to pick up your cars."

"I wish you didn't have to go." She sounded upset. "When will you be back in Paris?"

"Because of my workload, I can't answer that question, Emma. But you and Marti will be in perfect hands with my brother and Guy."

For the first time all evening he turned to Fleurine. She stood there wearing the same black dress she'd worn last evening. He thought she looked a little pale.

"Dennis will keep you and your mother well-informed about your father."

"Thank you for everything you've done for us, Raoul. We'll never forget your kindness." Her tone sounded genuine, but he heard no softness in her.

"This has been something our whole family has wanted to do for you and your family for a long time. Now I'll say good-night and a final *adieu*."

Just leave, Causcelle, and never look back. Don't gaze into my eyes that once upon a time revealed that my heart, body and soul were yours.

He strode down the hall to the elevator and went up to his suite. After getting ready for bed, he made a call to his pilot. The other call to his assistant on the estate kept him busy for another half hour while they discussed some problems needing solving. It helped him from turning inside out over Fleurine.

Knowing he'd sent Simone the picture he'd taken of her children the night before, he climbed under the covers to sleep. Then his cell rang. It was Jean-Louis checking in with him. He tapped to accept the call. "Don't you ever go to bed?"

His brother laughed. "Pascal seems to think you hit it off with his father's assistant tonight. With that red hair, she's one attractive woman, *frérot*."

"She is, but I lied to him so he wouldn't be disappointed until I told him the truth later."

His brother let out a groan. "I knew it! What kind of chemistry is it going to take? You need to move to the other side of the planet and start over."

"Never. With Dumotte headed for prison, home is where I'm staying for good. Think about it. Our father has been alone twenty-nine years. He could never replace our mother. I've been alone ten years and have decided I take after him. Like father, like son. Have a good night. You're the best. I'll call you tomorrow evening."

He hung up and buried his face in the pillow, praying for sleep.

His prayer wasn't answered. He relived that time on the estate when Fleurine had been the love of his life. His body thrashed around as he thought of old man Demotte, the monster who'd created the situation in which Raoul found himself at this very moment. Fleurine had undergone a seismic change, and there wasn't a damn thing he could do about it. What haunted him now was this darkness closing in on him, choking the very life out of him.

During the night, Fleurine was in so much agony over Raoul she couldn't sleep. His final words of goodbye played through her mind and body over and over again. When he'd used the word *adieu*, it felt as if a javelin had sliced her heart into a million pieces. Historically, the word *adieu* meant goodbye forever.

She hadn't used that word when she'd rejected him, but he'd internalized her goodbye that way. Tonight he'd used the word and he'd meant it because it had come from the depth of his being.

Unable to bear the pain of what she'd done and the hurt she'd caused him, she put on a robe and went in the other room not knowing where to turn. By tomorrow night she'd be sleeping at her apartment. That's when she heard quiet sobbing coming from the couch. "Emma?"

Her sister sat up. "Sorry. I didn't mean to waken you."

"You didn't. I couldn't sleep either. Why are you crying?"

"It doesn't matter."

"Of course it does." She sat down across from Emma. "Tell me what's wrong."

"I feel like a fool." Her voice trembled.

"Why?"

"You saw what happened earlier tonight. That woman came on the cruise with Raoul's cousin and wife and sat next to him. I thought I'd have time to really talk to him during dinner. I'd hoped to make some plans with him, but she took over and left me no chance. You heard what he said when he drove us here. He's leaving for La Racineuse in a few hours, and I don't know when I'm going to see him again. I can't stand it."

Neither can I.

"He runs the entire estate, Emma, yet has taken time out to look after our family after our father's arrest. Now he has to get back."

"I know. So I've been thinking about not going to the Sorbonne. I'd rather go home and keep working at the *fromagerie*. That way I'll be able to see him a lot and try to get him interested in me."

With those words, Fleurine got up from the

chair, unable to sit still. "You could do that, but do you really want to give up the opportunity of a lifetime?"

"You don't understand, Fleur. I've fallen in love with Raoul. It happened the second I met him. That may sound crazy to you, but I know it's real."

Fleurine's eyes closed tightly as she hugged her arms to her waist. "I believe you. In fact, I once had the exact same experience." The time had come to tell her sister the truth.

"Who was it?" Emma asked. "Why didn't you tell me about your old boyfriend when we were back at the house?"

"Because I wasn't ready to share. My love for this man began when we were in grade school on the estate. He was a year older than I. During recess we'd play together. Every school day I waited for recess like it was Christmas Day."

"How cute."

"He was the cutest boy at school. I dreamed about him every night."

"That sounds serious. I never felt like that about a guy until I was a senior and met Vince while I was walking past the hothouse on my way home from school. He was really cute too. We met there a few times, but someone told our father they'd seen us together talking. He forbade me from being anywhere around Vince since I'd be married soon to a man he'd chosen for me."

Fleurine shivered. "As horrible as that sounds, it's nothing compared to what happened to me."

"Tell me everything."

"My life centered on him. When he wasn't there, my day was ruined. I longed for middle school so we could begin having some classes together. My whole world turned to heaven the day we had a history class. We couldn't sit by each other, but he'd pass me notes. You'll never know how happy it made me.

"Pretty soon he'd be waiting for me on my way home from school. We'd talk by the fence until I had to go."

"Did you ever sneak off with him someplace?"

"Never. I was too afraid of our father. But the worst news came in secondary school when he told me that he had to leave the estate and go to college. I almost died hearing that news. He asked me to meet him at the hay barn where he worked so we could say goodbye."

"How awful he had to go away."

"You'll never know my pain. Anyway, I made him some *mannele* for a farewell gift and rode my bike to the barn. He took me and my bike inside and shut the barn door. It was the first time we'd ever been alone where no one could see us."

Emma sat up straighter. "What happened?"

"He started kissing me, then he proposed."

"He *what*?"

"His plan was to come back to the estate at Christmas. I would have just turned eighteen, and we could run away and get married. He promised to love me forever and take care of me. I'd never known such joy in this life, but it was short-lived."

"Why?"

Fleurine trembled. "Papa found out I was in there and opened the barn door. Worse, he held a rifle and aimed it straight at us."

"Oh, Fleur—"

"He said, 'Get your hands off my daughter or I'll shoot you dead this instant.'"

At that point Emma jumped off the couch and ran over to embrace her. "I can't even imagine how terrifying that must have been for you. I knew our father was crazy, but to threaten you!"

"It was truly horrifying, Emma. He ordered me to get in his truck outside. I started throwing up before he drove me home. I never knew what happened to the guy who'd proposed to me until later because Papa drove me to his sister's house in Switzerland that night. He spread the lie that I'd gotten married. Nothing could have been further from the truth."

"I remember Maman saying you'd gone away to get married. I didn't understand."

"How could you? I was kept prisoner there until Maman's money helped me escape on Christmas Day. She'd sent me a present and a note that said the boy I'd loved was fine. I was so thankful and took a train to Paris to start a new life where I changed my name legally. That way our father couldn't find me."

Emma stepped away from her. "That was ten years ago. Who was the guy, Fleur? You can't leave me hanging, not after everything you've told me."

Now came the difficult part. "Raoul."

In the dim light, Fleurine watched her sister's face crumble. Emma paced the floor for a minute, then whirled around. "The Raoul Causcelle we were with tonight?" Her cry resounded in the living room. "*He* asked you to marry him? Why in heaven's name didn't you tell me the second I told you how I felt about him?"

She took a deep breath. "Because it was past history. We hadn't seen each other in ten years, and our lives have gone in different directions. We're strangers to each other at this point."

Emma shook her head and stared at her. "I don't believe a love like that just disappears. It's probably the reason why he has never married *and* the reason he has been so good to our family. I couldn't understand why such an extraordinary, out-of-this-world man would do what he's done for us. Now it's making sense."

"Emma—"

"He's still in love with you, isn't he? Come on. Be honest."

Fleurine looked away. "After we accidentally met here in Paris and he found out I'd never married, he wanted to get back together. I told him it wasn't possible because we weren't the same people anymore. He had his life, and I had mine."

Her sister shook her head. "You mean you'd rather be in Paris working as a software engineer than be married to him? Are you insane?" Her voice rang out again. "I'd give anything on earth to meet such a fantastic man. I just wish I'd known about the two of you before I threw myself at him. I've made a fool of myself."

"No, you haven't, Emma. Don't ever think that. It's my fault." Fleurine knew she was hurting. "I should have said something back at the house before we flew here with him. But Maman told me to say nothing until the situation with our father had been resolved. My hands were tied."

"Well, there are no secrets now. I want to know how you saw him again here in Paris."

"Let's sit down, and I'll tell you everything."

For the next half hour, she explained the circumstances. When she'd finished, Marti suddenly appeared out of the woodwork.

He smiled. "At last I understand what's been going on since that detective drove us home from the *fromagerie*. Everyone working there has speculated about Raoul's single status. To think *you're* the woman Raoul loves! That's the coolest thing I ever heard. He's the best!"

"I found that out the day I met him years ago."

"No wonder he's remained single all these years, because you're the best too. So, what's stopping you? All that malarkey about being strangers is a crock. You fell in love as kids. That kind of love *never* goes away."

"Oh, Marti!" She hugged him hard. "My cruel rejection hurt him. He'll never forgive me."

"Want to bet? He didn't give us those cars and pay for four years of university for nothing!"

Fleurine moaned. "Our father was a monster, and Raoul and his family are the kindest people I've ever known to want to help us. But I don't want him to feel he owes us anything more."

Marti frowned. "Haven't you been listening? This isn't about us. He's head over heels in love with *you*. But if you're too stubborn to see it, then you don't deserve him."

"You don't know everything. Maman was

right when she told me that Raoul and I come from two different worlds."

"That's a ridiculous cliché, and you know it. If it's true, how come he proposed to you at eighteen? He wasn't blind to our world back then and knew exactly what he wanted when he pursued you."

"He's right," Emma chimed in. "Listen to our brother."

Marti moved closer. "The man asked you to meet him in secret while our father was still terrorizing everyone. Now it's a decade later. He's going to prison because of Raoul, who still wants you and lives on the estate. Why are you holding back on this?"

She got up from the couch. "I'm afraid I've hurt him too deeply."

"Then, there's only one way to find out. Go to him."

"Let's not talk about Raoul. Right now, I'm concerned about you guys. What do you say we go to bed for a few more hours? Tomorrow I'll take a taxi to my apartment and come back for you in my car by seven.

"We'll drive to the dealership so you can pick up your new cars. Then you can follow me to my apartment and have a look for yourself before you go to class. If you like it, then I'd love you to stay with me. Otherwise, I presume you'll decide on student housing, because you can't stay here. Try to get a little sleep now. I love you both so much. Emma, I hope you know I never meant to hurt you by withholding information."

"I get it, and I'll get over it because I love you too. Don't worry. It's not too late where Raoul is concerned, but don't wait too long."

"Emma's right," her brother said before going to his bedroom.

Sleep eluded Fleurine completely. The conversation had forced her to confront her feelings for Raoul. Were her brother and sister right? Did she still have a chance with Raoul? Or was her mother's advice true, and Fleur was right to keep Raoul at arm's length because it could never be? Those questions tortured her.

Early in the morning, she packed and called for a taxi. At six fifteen she went out in front. There was no sign of Raoul or his car, intensifying her pain. She left for her apartment. After grabbing a cola from the fridge, she got in her car and headed back to the *palais* to pick up her siblings and their belongings.

Within another hour they'd gone by the dealership to get their new cars and followed her to the apartment. They made the decision to stay with her for the time being, then they left for the university.

After they drove off, Fleurine lay down on the bed and phoned her mother.

"Maman, did you get the job at the *boulangerie*?"

"I did, and I'm working as we speak."

"That's the greatest news I could have. I'm so proud of you."

"It's a miracle. Do you know Raoul sent me a picture of all of you going to the Tour Eiffel for dinner? Talk about a happy family. He's one incredible man."

"He's the reason I'm calling you. Maman, something has happened you need to know about before you hear it from the kids. Can you talk?"

"I'm alone right now. Go ahead."

"They've gone to the university in their cars, but they'll be back at my apartment later. They're planning to stay with me for a while anyway."

"Wonderful! Now, tell me what is worrying you?"

In the next breath Fleurine told her about the situation with Emma and her crush on Raoul. When she'd finished, her mother chuckled.

"That poor thing, but she's only been under his influence two days. She still has time to get over it because she loves you. As for Raoul, he has that effect on every woman living. But you and he imprinted on each other in childhood. It's the reason he's never found another woman he could love."

Fleurine trembled. "That's the thing, Maman. I ended it with him in Ischia after he asked me to marry him again. I told him I couldn't because I loved my life as a software engineer and planned to go to the top. By telling him that, I hurt him so terribly he'll never be able to forgive me or let me in his life again."

After a long pause Simone said, "You told him that because of what I wrote to you in my letter ten years ago. I knew you were hurting, and I didn't want you to die of love for him. So I told you to make a success of your life and not depend on a man.

"Surely you know why I said what I did. But that man adores you to the point he's turned himself inside out for you and our family. If you'll go to him and explain the real reason you turned him down, he'll fall for you all over again."

Fleurine couldn't hold back to her tears. "Marti told me the same thing last night."

"I raised a brilliant son."

"I'm afraid it's too late."

"Nonsense. Not everyone in this life gets a second chance. If I could give you a mother's wisdom one more time, I'd tell you to come home to La Racineuse and make your life here where your love ignited. Like his brothers, Raoul's heart is here on the estate. He's never going to leave. If he sees you back and settled, he'll know you can't live without him either. That'll be the proof he needs to know you love him more than life itself."

With pounding heart, she sat up on the bed. "If I thought that were true… I'd have to resign from Aire-Tech."

"Then, what are you waiting for, *ma fille*?"

She was way ahead of her mother. "I'm so glad you could talk to me. Thank you for everything. Your advice saved me once. I have faith it will save me again if my love for Raoul is meant to be. Have I told you how thrilled I am about your new career? I'll call you later when I know my plans. I hope you don't mind my moving back in with you."

"It's your home too and always will be."

After getting off the phone, she freshened up and left in her car for Aire-Tech. No doubt her boss wondered what was going on with her. When she entered the building, she went straight to Philippe's office and peeked inside.

He smiled. "Laure! At last!"

"I know I've been gone longer than you'd anticipated, but so much has happened I hardly know where to start."

"Sit down, and let's talk."

She sat opposite him. "I have to tell you that no one has ever had a better, kinder, more understanding employer than you. I'll never be able to thank you enough for hiring me and giving me all the opportunities I've enjoyed over these past five years."

His smiled faded. "Why do I get the feeling you're about to quit on me?"

"I have to! In order to be with the man I love heart and soul, I have to move back east where I was born. It's where he was born too and works and lives. If I want to spend the rest of my life with him, I can't stay in Paris.

But please know I won't leave until you've found someone else."

"It will be difficult, if not impossible, to replace you."

"You know that's not true, but I love hearing you say it. I'm back right now and am ready to go to work until you've found the right person."

He sat forward. "From the beginning I've wondered why you weren't snapped up long ago. Now that I can feel your urgency and excitement, far be it from me to stand in the way of your happiness. If you want to clear out your office, you're welcome to leave as soon as tomorrow or the next day. I can tell you're in a hurry. He's a very lucky man."

Her eyes smarted. "Thank you, Philippe. You're the best, and I'll never forget you." She wrote out her address on the estate and handed it to him.

Fleurine left and went upstairs to her office to phone her landlords. She explained she had to leave Paris. However, her brother and sister were both attending the Sorbonne and would like to stay in her apartment. Fleurine offered to pay more rent for the two of them.

Her landlords sounded disappointed she

was leaving, but they were delighted to know her family would like to rent from them. With that decided, she gathered up her things and left the building. Thank goodness Paul had been working outside the office and hadn't seen her.

Relieved, she drove back to her apartment and started to pack. After so many years, she was finally going home where she'd always yearned to be. Her heart leaped when she thought of seeing Raoul again in such familiar surroundings. She clung to her mother's last comment.

If he sees you back and settled, he'll know you can't live without him either.

CHAPTER EIGHT

RAOUL HAD BEEN back on the estate more than two weeks, knee-deep in work. But no amount of business prevented thoughts of Fleurine from torturing him. How long would he remain in this hell which was becoming more unendurable by the second? While he'd been analyzing figures from the livestock report, Damond came into his office late one afternoon and put a small white bakery box on the desk.

He eyed his assistant. "What's this?"

"Before I left town, I decided to pick up a treat for us." He opened it and pulled out a *mannele* with chocolate bits on top and ate one. "Have you ever had one of these? They've just started making them, and I could eat a dozen of them in one go."

The sight of his favorite bread brought so much pain Raoul squeezed his eyes together for a moment. He pushed himself away from the desk and stood up so he could breathe. "Where did you buy them?"

"At Beauchamps. It's the only *boulangerie* in La Racineuse I like."

Raoul wheeled around. "Who waited on you?"

"Maureen, the owner. Who else? What's wrong? You look like you've seen a ghost."

Maybe he *was* losing his mind. "I've got to go, but I'll be back soon to eat the one you brought me. Thanks, Damond."

He raced out of his office to his truck and headed for town at top speed. Raoul had bought pastry from Beauchamps for years, but he'd never known them to make *mannele* bread, let alone with chocolate bits. Only one person in the world had ever produced one like that.

When he rolled up in front a few minutes later and got out, he saw the Closed sign in the window. Muttering a few choice epithets, he walked back to the truck and climbed in. After rubbing his eyes, he turned on the engine and started for the estate.

Before he went home for dinner, he returned to his office, deciding to eat the treat

Damond had bought him. He reasoned it couldn't possibly taste like Fleurine's and he'd be able to put this earthshaking incident to rest.

His assistant had gone home, leaving Raoul alone. He walked over to his desk and opened the box.

Here goes.

He reached inside.

One taste, and he was instantly transported back in time to the hay barn when he'd devoured Fleurine's parting gift. He swallowed it in two bites, wanting more. There could be no mistake. It meant that somehow the bakery had acquired a recipe like Simone's, the one Fleurine had learned from her mother.

Before he left for home, Raoul phoned Simone. He needed answers but reached her voice mail. He left a message that he needed to talk to her and asked her to call him back.

Once at the chateau he realized he had no appetite and went straight up to his suite. Raoul kept waiting for his phone to ring. It rang half a dozen times, all right, but nothing came from Simone. He finally climbed into bed. To his chagrin, restlessness kept him from getting a good sleep, and he awakened early. He planned to drive to the *boulangerie* before he showed up at his office.

"Raoul Causcelle!" a voice called to him as he entered twenty minutes later. "I haven't seen you in here for quite a while. What brings you around?"

He smiled at the owner. "*Bonjour*, Maureen. Last evening my assistant brought me some of your goodies. They were so delicious I've come back for more."

"That's good to hear. What would you like?"

"Your *mannele*. It has to be a new product you've introduced, and that bread happens to be one of my favorites."

"After all the years you've come in the bakery, I didn't realize you had a preference for it. You should have said something long before now. You'll be happy to hear my new pastry chef includes them in her repertoire."

"Anyone I know?"

"Simone Dumotte."

Simone? So he hadn't imagined it.

"When did you hire her?"

"About two weeks ago. It was after her husband's arrest. She's an outstanding pastry maker, and I was lucky to get her before she found work somewhere else. You remember Horace. He had to retire."

Raoul nodded. "Do you have any more *mannele* right now?"

"Sorry. They sold out so fast it was amazing. You're not the only one with a taste for it. Come by before we close this evening, and I'll have some boxed for you. How many do you want?"

"Save me a dozen." He pulled a bill out of his wallet and put it on the counter. "Thank you."

"*Bien sûr.* I'm glad you came by. It's nice to see you again. Have a great day."

"You too."

Raoul left and headed off for work. He couldn't get over Simone. That woman was something else. Already she'd become pastry chef of the best *boulangerie* in La Racineuse. She possessed a drive, the same drive she'd passed on to her daughter. After escaping to France from Switzerland, Fleurine had earned her living making bread and pastry so she could go to college. After doing a lot of research on what kind of career she wanted, she'd aspired to become a talented software engineer.

Untethered from Dumotte's leash, both she and her mother had been ready to conquer new worlds. Naturally he was thrilled Simone had refused to be a victim, but this new job had happened so fast! Evidently she'd wanted to be a pastry chef for years. All it took was getting rid of Garber to realize her dream.

Raoul had never seen that side in either of them. Except when he really thought about it, that wasn't true. Simone had helped Fleurine escape from her desperate situation years ago. In truth she'd methodically thought things out months before Christmas so Fleurine could get away, be safe and excel in a career she treasured more than anything else.

More than being with me.

Raoul's gut twisted. The Dumotte women were unstoppable. His head had been in the clouds where Fleurine was concerned.

At quarter after four that afternoon he left work for the *boulangerie* wanting to pick up the pastry his mouth watered for. But before driving away with it, he got in his truck and drove around the back. With the Renault still there, he waited in the cab for Simone to emerge from the rear exit.

As soon as she appeared, he got out and walked toward her. "Simone?"

"Oh, Raoul—*bonsoir!* I was planning to call you tonight. Last evening, I was out playing dominoes with my friends, and we all agreed to turn off our phones. Forgive me for not getting back to you sooner."

Simone already had a *coterie* of friends to enjoy. The knowledge warmed his heart.

"Don't think about that. I'm just glad I caught up to you. Maureen told me you'd been hired. Fleur always claimed you were the greatest cook on earth. Now you're the head pastry chef at Beauchamps. I'm proud of you."

"Thank you. I'm very happy. How are things for you?"

The woman had no idea the agony he was in. "I'm doing fine. What's new from Emma and Marti?"

"Lots of moans and groans while they catch up on several weeks of missed work. It's music to my ears, of course. Thanks to you and your family's incredible generosity, they're finally able to get the kind of education I've always wanted them to have. I swear

I'll never be able to repay you, but I'm going to try."

He shook his head. "We've been all through this before, Simone. It's your goodness and sacrifice that kept everyone safe all these years. Our family can never repay you enough. No amount of money could equal your courage. You have maintained a loving, stable home that kept Garber doing his job at the dairy until he was caught.

"Speaking of Garber, I just learned today that his sentencing will be next week. The attorneys working with me have urged the judge to bring it forward as soon as possible and get it over with. You won't be required to attend unless you want to."

"I couldn't, Raoul. I never want to see that man again."

"I understand completely."

A shudder racked her body. "He came close to murdering me when I was sixteen. Knowing this is about to end is the best news possible."

Raoul reached out and drew her into his arms. "Your nightmare is over." He could wish that his own would end. "Everyone on the estate is feeling the relief. Remember that if you need or want anything, all you have to do is call me. I'll always be here for you."

She kissed his cheek. "Bless you, Raoul."

After he helped her into her car, he started for home. At least the air was cooler now that October had come. He could be grateful for that much respite, even if he wondered how much longer he could endure this life. It angered him that thoughts of Fleurine still held him captive. What in the devil was wrong with him?

A week ago, Fleurine had driven to La Racineuse from Paris and had settled in with her mom. She felt good about leaving Emma and Marti. They'd met the landlord couple and seemed perfectly happy living in Fleurine's apartment while they went to the university.

One uncomfortable moment happened when Fleurine went back to Aire-Tech to get the last few personal items from her office. Paul had learned she was leaving and wanted to know why. She told him she missed home but thanked him for his friendship and wished him well. He didn't like her response and followed her out to her Peugeot in back. Poor Paul. He needed help. Hopefully the new female software engineer Philippe hired would fall for him.

"Fleur?"

Her mom had come home.

"I'm in the kitchen fixing dinner."

"Something smells good."

She smiled. "I hope you like chicken stir-fry. It's Deline's recipe. I used to make it a lot in Paris." She would miss her friend.

Her mother walked in. "I'm sure I'll love it, but first I've got fantastic news for you. Maureen said she'd be happy to hire you as a favor to me in order to help me. The job starts tomorrow."

Fleurine ran over and hugged her. "She must think the world of you."

"Since I was hired, my specialty breads have been selling out. That's what did the trick."

"I'm not the least bit surprised."

"Guess what's the best seller?"

"The cinnamon *stollen*?"

"You're close. It's the *mannele*."

"Raoul's favorite," she whispered.

"That's right. And I found out his assistant on the estate bought some yesterday."

Fleurine pressed her hands to her heart. "If Raoul happens to notice, he might co—"

"He already did, *ma fille*. Earlier this evening I discovered Raoul out in back of the *boulangerie* waiting for me in his truck."

A gasp escaped Fleurine's lips.

"He said he wanted to know why I hadn't returned his phone call because he had news about Garber. I lied and said I'd been out playing dominoes with my friends and turned off my phone."

"Uh-oh."

"Don't worry. He didn't mind, and he gave me the best news I could have heard. Your father will be facing the judge next week instead of months from now. That's all because of Raoul and his family's influence. It won't be long before he begins his prison sentence."

"That's a miracle."

"It is." Her mother wiped her eyes. "But another one is about to happen too."

"What do you mean?"

"He recognized my recipe for *mannele*. The next time he comes to get more because he can't resist, he'll find out you're working there too. Anything can happen after that."

Fleurine took a shaky breath. "Still, you don't know the damage I've done to him."

"I think I do. He asked about Marti and Emma but didn't mention you while we talked. That was the surest sign he's still fighting to get over you. I know it's not too late. You came home in time to fix this situation."

"I don't have your faith, Maman."

She put her hands on her hips. "The fact that you're home, working in the *boulangerie*, of all places, instead of solving software problems in Paris will once again upend his universe. This time with the right results. Mark my words."

"I'm going to pray for that."

"We both will. Now, I'm hungry. Let's eat."

Mid-October brought Raoul and his brothers to the courtroom of the Ministry of Justice for criminal proceedings in Paris. The day they'd all been waiting years for had arrived. Fleurine's father would be sentenced for crimes committed against the monks of the Church, the property, his family and Raoul.

The judge read each charge. After he'd finished, he ordered the defendant to stand. "It's the finding of this court that Garber Dumotte will receive consecutive life sentences and be remanded to La Santé Prison in Paris, without the possibility of parole."

At that pronouncement, the three brothers hugged each other before they embraced Claude Giraud and George Delong, the two men who'd helped put Garber away.

Raoul watched old man Dumotte being led out of the courtroom in ankle chains and handcuffs. As wretched a creature as he was, he had to remember that Garber happened to be Fleurine's father.

When the side door closed behind Garber, Raoul felt it as if a sonic boom had pronounced the end of an era. Now a new one was beginning, but he didn't know what that looked like. Today they would fly home and let their father know the outcome. Beyond that, all Raoul could do was take it one day at a time.

They took a limo to the airport and left for home. By evening their father and the whole family had gathered around the dining room table to hear what had gone on in court. After Raoul had given an account, he turned the conversation over to his father, who had the last word before dinner was served.

"I'm grateful this day has come, and I only have one thing to say. We reap what we sow. Let us all try to sow the best of ourselves."

"Amen," everyone murmured, and they started eating.

Corinne eyed Raoul. "Nic said that none of the Dumotte family were in court for the sentencing today, not even Fleur who'd helped give earlier testimony against her father."

Raoul had to clear his throat. "That's right. Simone told me last week that it would be too painful for all of them."

"I can't even imagine it," Yvette interjected. "Come to think of it, my friend Marie said she saw Fleur at the Beauchamps *boulangerie* in La Racineuse yesterday. I thought she lived and worked in Paris."

Raoul almost dropped his cup of coffee. He wished to heaven his sisters would get off the subject of Fleurine, but it was impossible. "She does. Marie had to be mistaken."

"No," she argued. "Marie said she heard someone call her name, but after ten years she hardly recognized her because she's absolutely gorgeous."

Anne, another Causcelle sister, nodded. "Fleur and her sister are lovely girls."

His brothers flashed Raoul private messages of commiseration. The news that Fleurine was on the estate had taken the three of them by surprise, and they knew he was in pain. Certainly, he hadn't had any idea she'd come home.

No doubt she'd wanted to keep her mother company during the sentencing. It made sense that she'd visit her at work. Raoul reasoned that in a day or two Fleurine would be back in Paris. Once she'd left, he'd check on Simone.

No longer able to tolerate sitting there with Fleurine the subject of conversation, he got up from the table. "If you'll all excuse me, I'm afraid I have a backlog of work to deal with before bed."

Once outside the chateau, he got in his car and found himself headed for the office. But halfway there, he made a left turn toward the Dumotte house. Fleurine had probably flown here or taken the train. He was crazy to go by there when he wouldn't be able to see her.

Nor did he want to.

Her rejection would haunt him to the grave.

Soon he came to the road in question and slowed down.

What in the hell was he doing?

Had he gone out of his mind?

In the next breath he started to turn his car around. That's when he spotted a green Peugeot parked behind Simone's Renault. He slammed on his brakes.

Fleurine had driven here?

Why would she do that?

With his torment off the charts, he took off for his office. It was the only place where he could have a meltdown in private and attempt to catch up on a ton of work. He'd put everything on hold because of Fleurine, but he couldn't allow himself to flounder any longer.

While on the jet flying home, he and Nic had volunteered to help on the construction of the house Jean-Louis and Françoise were building on the property. Between that project and his estate work, it would keep him busy and save his life for a while longer. Beyond that he didn't dare speculate.

A week later Raoul had to go to town on an errand and decided to drop by the *boulangerie* to see Simone. to his frustration, Maureen wasn't there, and a salesclerk he didn't recognize told him it was Simone's day off. Not about to be put off, he would run by her house on the way home.

"May I help you?"

"Please. I'd like a dozen *mannele*."

"They disappear as fast as they're made. I'll see if there are any more in back."

While he checked his phone messages, the woman returned to the counter. He lifted his head and found himself staring into a pair of violet eyes he could never get enough of. His heart thundered. "*Fleurine!* What are you still doing in town? Why are you wearing that apron?"

Her expression fell, as if she were upset by what he'd said. "You *knew* I've been here?"

"Yes." He fought a losing battle with his emotions. "At dinner last week my sister told me her friend saw you in here. How's your mother?"

She bit her lower lip, drawing his attention to her exquisite features and that mouth he craved waking or sleeping. "Doing better than I could have imagined."

He shifted his weight. "Are you all right now that your father has gone to prison?"

"Like Maman, I've never been happier, knowing he can never hurt any of us again."

This was agony. "Our family will be glad to know how you feel."

"But not *you*?" She sounded devastated, and her unexpected question felt like a stab.

"What do you mean?"

A look of sadness crossed over her face. "You've known I've been here for over a week, but you never came in."

He couldn't figure her out. "What's going on with you, Fleurine? We said our goodbyes in Ischia. I made a promise. Why would I come near you at this point?"

She avoided his gaze. "You wouldn't, and of course you'd have every reason not to. But I'll admit I've been praying every day that you'd walk in here. You see, I've been hired as Maman's assistant pastry chef."

Her admission came at him like a bolt of lightning. "You mean she asked you to help her?"

"No. I resigned from Aire-Tech and have moved home for good."

He ran trembling hands through his hair, trying to assimilate what she'd just said. "That means you've come because your mother is ill."

"No, Raoul," she countered. "This is a permanent move on my part for my own reasons."

Beyond bewildered, he stared hard at her. "Then, it's *you* who is ill. Otherwise you wouldn't be here. Do you have cancer or something else life-threatening and need her to care for you? All you have to do is let our family know and we'll cover the cost."

Tears filled those glorious eyes. "Only you would say that, because you're the most generous man in existence. I don't have cancer. It's something much more serious. Worse, there's just one treatment to cure what's wrong."

His body grew cold. "What are you saying?" He was ready to explode in pain.

"Look… I'm still working and can't talk about it right now. In fact, I shouldn't have said anything at all. I'm so sorry I did." She started to turn away.

"Oh, no, you don't, Fleurine!"

She stopped in her tracks and looked back at him.

"You can't drop a bomb like that and leave me to disintegrate."

Tears filled her eyes. "That's the last thing I meant to do."

There it was…that old sweetness. But he refused to be taken in again.

"I want an explanation, Fleurine. I'll go around the back of the *boulangerie* so you can let me in."

"Don't do that, please," she begged. Wringing her hands she said, "Since the *mannele* won't be ready until later today, I promise to bring it to you when I'm off work. Tell me where, and I'll be there."

His hands formed fists. "How do I know you'll keep your promise?"

"I—I guess you don't," she said uncertainly. "But if you knew the truth, you'd understand that my whole life depends on talking to you about what's wrong."

"*Now* what are you saying?" He couldn't take any more.

"Shh! People can hear us. You have to leave," she whispered. "I swear I'll meet you wherever you say."

He didn't have to think. "Come to my office at seven. We'll be alone." His office had turned into his cave.

"I'll be there. Honestly, I will." She kept swallowing hard. "Thank you."

Fleurine hurried back to the kitchen, so excited she felt sick because she'd be seeing Raoul at the end of the day. But on the heels of her euphoria came fear because she'd done such a thorough job of pushing him away. How would he ever be willing to listen to her and understand why she'd said those cruel things to him?

She'd treated Raoul like a child who'd played with a favorite toy until she didn't want it anymore and carelessly threw it away. Fleurine was mortified by what she'd done. The only reason he'd agreed to meet with her after work was because he believed she was on the verge of dying.

Fleurine worked hard for the rest of the day, struggling not to break down. Tonight would be her one and only chance to lay her heart at his feet. But the question remained. Could she truly expect him to want her after the way she'd thrown his proposal back in his face? Her father hadn't been the only monster living in the Dumotte home.

When the time came for her to leave work,

she flew out the back door with a box of *mannele* and drove straight home.

"Maman?"

"I'm in the bedroom!"

With tears gushing, she rushed in and flew into her mother's arms. "Raoul came in to the *boulangerie* and found out I worked there. I'd hoped he would realize why I'd come home and be convinced I'd given up everything for love of him." She shook her head. "Nothing could have been further from the truth."

"Why do you say that?"

"When he learned I gave up my job and had been here over a week without telling him, he jumped to the conclusion I'd come home because *you* were terminally ill."

"*What?*"

"Of course I told him no. That's when he assumed that *I'm* the one battling an incurable disease and came home so you could take care of me! But here's the amazing part." More tears flowed. "Even though I know he'll never take me back, he still offered to pay the medical costs."

"That Raoul is a saint, but what he said still doesn't sound like a man who has lost all hope."

"His innate goodness has nothing to do with love. He came to earth that way."

"I agree."

"Maman, I was dying to tell him everything right then, but I couldn't talk with customers around. He assumed I'd been talking about an illness, and he wouldn't leave. I could tell he didn't believe me, and I begged him to go. I promised to meet him later and explain. When he still hesitated, I told him that my whole life literally depended on being able to talk to him about my condition, but it had to be in private."

"That poor man must be twisted in knots."

"No, Maman. I'm the one in that state. He finally told me to come to his office at seven, but I can't imagine him wanting to start over with me again after what I've done."

Her mother patted her arm. "In that case there's only one thing to do. Since you started this by coming home from Paris in the first place, you have to be the one to end it. No matter your fear of the outcome, I suggest you honor your promise to him this evening and bare your soul. You owe him that much."

"I owe him everything," she said, her voice shaking.

"He needs to hear that. It's the only way either of you is going to get on with your lives." Her mother glanced at her watch. "You'd better hurry if you're supposed to be there by seven."

Fleurine dashed into the bathroom to shower and wash her hair. Later, as she stood in front of the mirror to style it, she remembered that afternoon years ago when she'd gone to the barn to meet Raoul. She'd wanted to look beautiful for him but had been forced to wear one of those awful dresses and leave her hair long. No makeup, no perfume.

This evening she would pull out all the stops, hoping to erase his Cinderella image of her. At five to seven she was ready to leave wearing a new knee-length sky-blue dress ruched at the waist with three-quarter sleeves. Her heart raced so hard she felt sick.

She found her mother in the kitchen and gave her a kiss. "Pray for me, Maman."

"I've never stopped. Neither should you."

CHAPTER NINE

SEVEN MINUTES AFTER SEVEN. Fleurine wasn't coming.

Unable to take anymore, Raoul shot up from his desk. Who knew what was wrong with her. He couldn't handle it right now. The only thing to do was leave La Racineuse and move to the other side of the planet as Jean-Louis had suggested.

He flew out the main door and headed for his truck parked in front. But he'd only made it halfway when a blue Renault pulled up behind it. He came to a stop.

Simone? Something serious must have happened. His heart almost failed him.

As the driver's door opened, a shapely female vision in soft blue emerged. In the twilight he realized it was Fleurine! *Grâce à Dieu.* She hurried toward him, and he caught the flowery fragrance of her perfume in the night breeze.

"Thank you for still being here. I know I'm late. Please don't leave." Her heavenly eyes implored him. "I was afraid you'd think I wasn't coming." She looked in perfect, amazing health but sounded out of breath. "My car wouldn't start so I had to bring my mother's, the one you gave her."

He rubbed the back of his neck. "It's growing cooler, and you're not wearing a coat."

"I didn't want one because I was in too big a hurry to talk to you."

Raoul made an instant decision. "I'd rather not go back in the office in case Damond decides to do some work. Let's drive to the chateau where we'll both be more comfortable."

A look of alarm broke out on her gorgeous face. "The chateau?"

"Yes. My suite is like an apartment. Since you have something extremely serious to confide in me, we won't be disturbed there by anyone. We'll enter through a side entrance so no member of the family will be aware."

"I appreciate that."

"Follow me." He walked to his truck and started the engine while she got back in her mother's car. Through the rearview mirror he watched as they headed for his home. For years he'd longed for the day when she'd step inside the place where he'd always lived. He never imagined it would happen at a time when she would tell him the one thing that was worse than her rejection of him. Never had he needed strength of the kind necessary to get through this next hour.

He drove around the side and parked by the side door. This entrance gave him easy access to his suite. He walked over and opened it as Fleurine pulled up next to him. After getting out, she followed him inside and up the stairs to the second floor.

Raoul walked down the hall and opened his suite door. "After you, Fleurine." She entered the foyer but seemed hesitant to go farther. "Why don't you go on through and sit on the couch."

"Thank you."

Her behavior confused him. She seemed wary rather than assertive, more like the old Fleurine. Her illness must be changing her in ways he was still trying to understand.

"Can I get you a drink?" he asked as she

sat on one end of the sofa. "Do you need anything?"

She shook her head and looked at him with pleading eyes. "I don't need anything except the chance for a final talk with you."

Final. He groaned. At this point he sank down on a chair across from her and leaned forward with his hands on his knees. "After what you told me at the *boulangerie*, I haven't thought about anything else. Why don't you just say it and get it over with. How much longer do you have to live?"

She jumped up and walked around for a moment before standing in front of him. "Raoul—" she spread her arms as if in exasperation "—I'm not dying! I tried to explain earlier at the *boulangerie*, but there were too many people around."

"But you said—"

"I said that my only cure would be to talk to you, but it didn't mean it had anything to do with the physical."

Raoul's hands slid to his face before he lifted his head to stare at her. "So you're saying that you're *not* dying?"

"Yes, I am, but it's because... I'm dying of love for *you*!"

Shocked and confused, he got to his feet, convinced he was having an hallucination like before. "Fleurine—"

"Let me finish. I gave up my job and have moved back here for good because I've loved you from childhood, and that has never changed. It's true, my darling. I love you more than life itself, but I know I've killed every ounce of feeling you've ever had for me because of my cruelty. Everything I said to you in Paris and Ischia was a complete lie!"

Reeling, he took several breaths. "But why?"

"My reason stems from the words my mother wrote to me in that letter inside my winter coat ten years ago. Maman put the fear of my father into me to keep us both safe. She knew he'd threatened to kill us, and she didn't want me to go back to you and endanger us.

"Being the wonderful mother she was, she understood I might die over losing you, so she urged me to escape and become successful through work. She counseled me to live a happy, fulfilled life without a man. That meant you. I determined to follow her counsel and tried not to look back. But then you and I met accidentally at Aire-Tech, and from that moment on, my life has been pure torture."

"*Torture* is the word, all right," he ground out.

"You'll never know how much I've hated myself for pushing you away, convinced I was doing the right thing. But then everything got worse when I realized Emma was falling in love with you."

He frowned. "Emma?"

"I couldn't let that go on another second and sat her down to tell her you were and are the great and only love of my life. She never knew about us, and when I watched her fall for you the moment she met you, I couldn't handle it. You were so wonderful to her, my jealousy turned me inside out."

"But you *couldn't* have been jealous. She's your sister!"

"You can't comprehend how much I've suffered since seeing you again. I've been halfway out of mind and not thinking clearly. That day when you came in my office and we saw each other for the first time in ten years, I wanted to fly into your arms and hold onto you for dear life. I wanted to tell you I'd marry you that very instant. I still want to be your wife and love you until the day I die and beyond, Raoul. I want children with you. Everything! That's what I came here to tell you."

No one had ever told Raoul you could die of a heart attack from too much joy.

"I know you despise me for everything I've said and done, Raoul, so I'll leave. You have my promise that I'll stay out of your way now that I'm living here and planning to find computer work. Just so you know, I'm not really working at Beauchamps. Maman arranged for that so you would eventually find out I was working there. I prayed the *mannele* would lure you there. I needed to talk to you but was afraid to approach you."

Raoul shook his head again. "I don't believe what I'm hearing."

"I'm sure you don't, and if you tell me you want me to leave La Racineuse and never come back, I'll be on the next plane out. But you deserved to hear the truth from me first. Thank you for giving me this much time."

His adorable Fleurine was back and so damn sweet he was melting on the spot. She started to head for the foyer, but Raoul raced in front of her and put his hands on her upper arms. "You're not going anywhere."

Her head flew back, revealing the stunned expression in those violet eyes that looked at him with pure love.

"We have wedding plans to make, *mon amour*."

The love and desire licking through those impossibly black eyes consumed her so completely, Fleurine had no words. She slid her arms around his neck, bringing their bodies together. He lowered his dark head and his compelling mouth found hers. This was no experimental kiss like the one in the barn. So great was their need to express their love, they came close to engulfing each other.

She lost track of time as they tried to become one, imprinting on each other, heart, body and soul. No dreams would ever match the reality of being in his strong arms again. "Darling," she moaned in ecstasy, "I love you. I love you so terribly it frightens me."

"You don't begin to know the meaning of fright. When you walked out of my suite at the *palais* declaring there was no us, I died inside."

"So did I, but that will never happen again."

Ravenous for him after being deprived all these years, she covered his mouth with her own.

Once again he swept her away with over-powering passion. "How have I existed this long without you?" he cried much later, finally giving her a chance to breathe.

"It's a miracle we're still alive at all," she whispered against his lips.

"That's why we need to be married. I'm calling Father Didier right now. It's not too late." He picked her up like a bride and carried her back to the couch, kissing her with a hunger that matched her own. After sitting down with her ensconced in his lap, he eventually relinquished her mouth long enough to pull out his phone and call the church.

She buried her face in his neck. "How do you have his number?"

"I've talked to him many times about you and your father."

Fleurine nestled closer, kissing his jaw. "I had a long talk with my priest in Paris before I flew here. He knows of my deep heart-ache over you." She half lay in his arms in a euphoric trance while he made the call. Her heart thrilled to the pure happiness in his voice as he asked the priest to marry him and Fleur Dumotte right away. More jubilant conversation ensued before he hung up and pulled her closer.

"Father Didier said it was long overdue that at least one of the Causcelle triplets took his vows in the cathedral. We will have a ceremonial blessing after a civil marriage. He'll officiate any time we want because our marriage takes priority over everything."

His mouth captured hers and they clung in the kind of rapture she could never have imagined before this moment. Their wedding really was going to happen. He'd be the husband she would love and cherish forever.

"*Mon trésor*," he murmured, covering her face with kisses, "the only thing I want to do is take you in the bedroom and make love to you forever. But I want you to be my wife before I hide you away from the world and keep you to myself. What do you say we go downstairs so Papa can meet you in person? We'll tell him our news, then go to your house and inform your mother she's getting a new son-in-law. If it were up to me, we'd get married first thing in the morning."

"I'd give anything if we could." On fire for him, she kissed him hungrily, never wanting to leave his arms. A few minutes later they let go of each other long enough to stand up.

He kissed her again. "Wait here one second."

She stood there in a daze until he returned and grasped her left hand. "This ring has been sitting on top of my dresser since Ischia."

A cry escaped her throat as he slid a gold ring with a two-karat violet stone onto her ring finger. "Oh, Raoul, it's the most incredible diamond I've ever seen."

"I finally found the one I wanted to give you that comes close to the color of your eyes. It comes from the Argyle Diamond Mine in Australia, which is one of the only sources of violet diamonds in the world."

"I didn't know one like this existed!" She launched herself in his arms again, unable to contain her love for him.

He cupped her face and kissed her. "We're finally engaged. I will never be separated from you again, my darling, but if you want to pursue your career in tech or be the finest baker in all of France, then you have my support. As long as you are by my side while you do it."

"Oh, darling! I want more than anything

else to be your wife and the mother of your children. Beyond that maybe I could find a software-engineer position in La Racineuse or work at the *boulangerie*. All I know is I never want to be separated from you again."

"That's all I needed to know. Now I'm going to phone Luca, my father's health-care nurse. If Papa's still awake, I want him to hear our news."

While she repaired her hair and lipstick, he pulled out his cell phone. Seconds later, he hung up and said, "Let's go." Putting his arm around her shoulders, they left his suite. He walked her down the hallway in the other direction leading to the main staircase. Her eyes took in the magnificent chateau interior. Soon they walked down another hall and entered another suite.

Fleurine saw Luca standing next to Raoul's father in a wheelchair. The older man had dressed in pajamas and a robe. His lively brown eyes darted to the two of them in surprise.

"Papa? Forgive us for coming this late, but my news can't wait."

As they drew closer, he broke out in a broad smile. "Well, well, well. Little Fleur Dumotte, all grown-up. You were the cutest little girl. It's no wonder my Raoul started following you around."

His words touched her heart. "Monsieur Causcelle, it's a privilege to finally meet you. I'll never be able to thank you enough for all you've done for me and my family."

"*Ma chère fille*, I had no idea what you and your family had been through until recently. I'm thankful all of you have survived and done so well."

Tears filled her eyes. "Everyone is more than fine, all due to your incredible generosity and goodness."

Raoul kept his arm around her shoulders. "Papa, tonight my Fleurine agreed to be my wife. You're the first to know."

His father's eyes watered. "Now my every prayer has been answered. Come here, Fleurine. Let me welcome you to the family." He held out his arms, and they embraced. "Finally my son is going to be happy again."

"We want to be married as soon as we can, Papa."

"Then don't let anything stop you."

"Father Didier will marry us in the cathedral."

"At last, we can all meet there together. Please let me offer the chateau for your wedding reception. The ballroom is large enough to hold all our families and friends."

Raoul hugged him. "That's my wish, *mon père*." He turned to Fleurine and kissed her cheek. "Would you like that, *chérie*?"

"I can't think of another place to hold it. This is your home and legacy. My mother will be overjoyed."

His father clapped his hands. "Joy has finally come back to the estate. I can die a happy man."

"Oh, please—don't say that!" Fleurine cried.

"We expect you around for many years, Papa. Now, if you'll excuse us, we're going to drive to Simone's house."

He eyed Fleurine. "Give her my very best and tell her to call me."

"I will, and thank you again. You've raised the most wonderful son on earth."

Raoul led her out and down another hall to the side door of the chateau. After another kiss to die for, they parted long enough to drive the short distance to her home. Fleurine was so happy she felt like they were floating on clouds.

"Maman?" she called to her when they entered the house.

"I'm coming!" She rushed in the living room from the kitchen. "Oh, Raoul—"

"Simone!" He let go of Fleurine and hugged her mother. "You don't know how long I've wanted to tell you how much I love your daughter. Tonight she agreed to be my wife. We want your blessing."

Tears ran down her cheeks. "You've always had it and should have been married years ago."

He shook his head. "None of that matters now. We're going to enjoy the rest of our lives now as man and wife. And you and Marti and Emma are going to be my family too."

Fleurine couldn't contain all the happiness building inside her. She ran to the two of them and threw her arms around both of them.

Her mother whispered, "He found out you couldn't live without him…"

La cathédrale in La Racineuse,
one week later

At twelve noon, Raoul waited impatiently outside the entrance of the *cathédrale* with his brothers. They were surrounded by the whole Causcelle family while they waited for the limo that would bring Fleurine and her family. Their wedding day was being celebrated not only as a marriage but a day of liberation and healing. A huge crowd of estate workers had assembled outside.

"Settle down, cousin. The limo has rounded the corner."

Grâce à Dieu.

"What would I have done without you all these years, Pascal? No man ever had a better friend."

"Ditto."

Another few seconds and Raoul hurried toward the place where the limo rolled to a stop. A chorus of *aah*s resounded when he opened the rear door and Fleurine stepped out on the cobblestones. In her flowing white wedding gown and long lace veil, she looked like a vision from heaven.

"My love," he whispered and grasped her hand as they made their way to the cathedral entrance. She carried her bridal bouquet of white roses in her other hand. He could hear the music inside as the doors opened. Father Didier, dressed in his ceremonial vestments, greeted them with a beautiful smile. He bade them follow him, and the processional began.

Everyone filed behind to fill the nave for the matrimonial mass. Raoul squeezed Fleurine's hand. She squeezed back harder, delighting him. They'd had a lot to do to prepare for this day. He'd purposely kept busy so he wouldn't kidnap her ahead of time and love her into oblivion. He had trouble believing that this day had finally arrived.

The priest turned and faced them. Emma stepped forward to relieve Fleurine of her bouquet, then he put up his hands. "In the name of the father, son, and holy spirit, grace to all of you and peace from God our father and the Lord Jesus Christ.

"Dearly beloved, you have come together into the house of the church so that your intention to enter into marriage may be strengthened by the Lord with a sacred seal.

"Christ abundantly blesses the love that binds you. Through a special sacrament, he enriches and strengthens those he has already consecrated by holy baptism, that you may be enriched with his blessing. And so, in the presence of the church, I ask you to state your intentions.

"Raoul Causcelle, have you come here to enter into marriage freely and wholeheartedly?"

"I have."

"Fleur Dumotte, have you come here to enter into marriage freely and wholeheartedly?"

"I have." Her voice sounded strong and clear.

"Since it is your intention to enter the covenant of holy matrimony, join your right hands and declare your consent before God and his church."

Raoul reached for hers with eagerness.

The priest sprinkled holy water on their rings before handing them over. "Raoul, repeat after me. Fleur Dumotte, receive this ring as a sign of my love and fidelity. In the name of the father, son, and holy spirit. Then put the ring on her finger."

Never had he wanted to do anything more than claim Fleurine for his own.

"Now Fleur, repeat after me. Raoul Causcelle, receive this ring as a sign of my love and fidelity. In the name of the father, son, and holy spirit."

Fleurine's fingers trembled as she slid home the gold ring she'd bought for him.

The priest smiled. "Now repeat after me. I, Raoul Ronfleur Causcelle, take you Fleur Binoche Dumotte, to be my wife. I promise to be faithful to you in good times and in bad, in sickness and in health, to love you and to honor you all the days of my life."

Turning to her, he repeated the vow that came from his soul.

The priest eyed Fleurine. "Now repeat after me. I, Fleur Binoche Dumotte, take you, Raoul Ronfleur Causcelle, to be my husband. I promise to be faithful to you, in good times and in bad, in sickness and in health, to love you and to honor you all the days of my life."

Fleurine's response thrilled him to the depths of his being.

"May the Lord in his kindness strengthen the consent you have declared before the church. What God has joined, let no one put asunder. May the God of Abraham, Isaac, Jacob, and the God who joined together our first parents in paradise strengthen and bless in Christ the consent you have declared before the church, so that what God joins together, no one may put asunder.

"In the sight of God and these witnesses, I now pronounce you husband and wife! You may now kiss."

Those violet eyes that had ensnared him as a young man gazed at him with so much love he trembled before lowering his mouth. No bride could ever have been more beautiful than Fleurine was to him. His brothers had warned him to be careful in front of a full audience of people. Somehow he managed not to devour her until the mass was over and they'd left the church to walk outside past the cheers of the crowd.

The bells rang out, proclaiming their joy as Raoul helped Fleurine into the rear of the waiting limo. Once they started moving, he pulled her into his arms. "Madame Causcelle... How long I've waited to be able to call you that."

"Not as long as I've waited to hear it, my darling Monsieur Causcelle." Their mouths fused in passion, and she received the husband's kiss she'd been dying for. They didn't come up for air until they reached the chateau fifteen miles away.

The limo parked in front of the entrance.

"Beloved," he murmured against her lips, "all we have to do is get through the toasts. Once the helicopter arrives on the grounds, we'll escape to Ischia and blot out the world."

Her heart leaped in response. "You're taking us there?"

"Where else?" Giving her another kiss, he opened the door to help her out of the back seat and escorted her inside with her bouquet.

"Oh, Raoul," she gasped when they reached the ballroom, clinging to him. "Your sisters and mine have transformed this gorgeous room into a fairyland. Look at all the trees and tiny white lights!"

Her gaze took in the many round tables covered with fine écru-colored linen, baskets of white roses and candelabras. The rectangular head table on one side of the room featured two wedding cakes on either end. They were stunning replicas of the Château Causcelle. Her mother had truly outdone herself. She'd put small bride and groom figurines on top of both.

"Look, Raoul! Maman managed to affix a picture of our faces over the faces of the dolls. Can you believe it?"

His smile made her legs go weak. "My

mother-in-law is not only an *artiste* she's one incredible woman who gave birth to the most amazing woman on earth. We'll have to save them for our children."

Their children...

He caught Fleurine to him and kissed her unabashedly in front of their guests who had filled the room and were taking their places.

She heard the sound of someone tapping the side of a goblet to get everyone's attention. The room quieted down as Raoul swept her along to the center of the head table. Once they were seated, Pascal stood up looking fabulous.

All the men in the wedding party including Marti, Raoul's father, brothers and brothers-in-law wore black tuxedos with flowers in the lapels. She looked around, but no one could match her new husband who always appeared drop-dead gorgeous no matter what he wore.

"Dear family and friends, my Oncle Louis asked me to greet all of you. We're honored to have Father Didier seated at the table with us on this red-letter day for Raoul and Fleur. He's been a comfort and friend to the Causcelle family and everyone on the estate.

"All of you who want to say a kind word

to Fleur or embarrass Raoul will be given the chance later." A roar of laughter went up. "First let me say that Raoul and I became good friends when we were little and our fathers worked together. I never had so much fun in my life as I had with him.

"I never saw a man more in love than he was during his teens. Then he and Fleur became separated. Raoul and I have seen each other through thick and thin. It got pretty thin for him over the last ten years. Then he accidentally saw Fleur again, and a miracle happened that spread light over the whole estate. Fleur returned, and my cousin hasn't stopped grinning ever since." More smiles came from the crowd. "Enjoy this remarkable moment in time. *Bon appétit.*"

The food turned out to be a divine feast, but since they'd taken their vows Fleurine couldn't have told anyone what she'd eaten. She kept glancing at Raoul in disbelief that they were actually married. In the midst of her reverie about him, Pascal got to his feet once more.

"Before the cutting of the wedding cakes, Louis would like to make a toast." He handed the microphone to Raoul's father who remained in his wheelchair.

"My wife and I were young like Fleur and Raoul when we fell in love. Fortunately for us, we were able to marry in our late teens and were blessed with six beautiful children. On the night before our triplet boys were born, we talked about the great responsibility and joy ahead of us.

"So much has happened since that moment. Today I'm surrounded by all my children and their spouses and my grandchildren. Of course I'm expecting more." Raoul winked at her. "Can you believe I'm still alive? My cup runneth over. Raoul and Fleur's marriage fulfills the culmination of every dream.

"I only have one more dream, and that is for all of us one day to be united with my beloved wife, Delphine…their mother and grandmother. Thank you all for making this the perfect day."

He raised his wineglass. "I propose a toast to Raoul and Fleur. May you cherish every moment of your lives from here on out."

The breeze off the Mediterranean filtered from the upstairs patio into the bedroom toward morning. Raoul had taken his father's last wish to heart. In the last twelve hours he and Fleurine had become the lovers of Raoul's dreams. But the reality of making love to his adorable wife went beyond any expectations his mind could have conceived. They would never be able to get enough of each other. There was no end to her giving. He couldn't bear the thought of ever being alone again. He needed her like he needed air to breathe.

Ten years of hunger couldn't be satisfied in one divine wedding night. He thanked heaven they had the rest of their lives to show each other what it meant to lie entangled in each other's arms day and night and pour out their love. Her beauty enchanted him inside and out. They'd brought each other intense pleasure over and over again.

He particularly loved the curve of her luscious mouth that drove him crazy whether waking or sleeping as she was now. He kissed her cheeks and hair, the curve of her brows and the tender spot in her throat where a nerve throbbed. She moved closer to him, brushing her hand over his upper arm without realizing it. Her touch, her innate sweetness, overwhelmed him. Unable to hold back, he began kissing her mouth awake.

"Darling," she murmured and started to respond. He pulled her over so she half lay on top of him. Within seconds the whole wonderful ritual began again. The next time he became aware of their surroundings, the sun had come streaming in from the patio.

"Good morning, *mon épouse*."

She opened her violet eyes and gazed at him with love. "Do you have any idea what you've done to me? How you've changed my whole life? I'm not the same person."

"Yes, you are. You're my precious Fleurine who enslaved me the first time I ever looked at you and heard your gentle laugh. I've never been the same since. You're all I've ever wanted. I'm so in love with you. Help me."

She smiled. "What do you mean?"

"I don't know exactly. I can't explain what I'm feeling."

Fleurine kissed his mouth. "I feel just like you. It's as if my love for you is exploding inside me. The solution is to hold onto each other for dear life."

"You don't have to worry about that," he cried.

They clung to each other. "We had the perfect wedding, Raoul."

"Amen. Even if we missed the first ten years, we're going to have the perfect life forever. We vowed to deal with the good and the bad times because our love will see us through anything."

"It already has. Look where we are now. I'm in your arms where I've always wanted to be. I'm the luckiest woman on the face of the earth. I love you, Raoul Causcelle."

"I love you, Fleurine Causcelle. I'm the happiest man on the planet. Come here to me and never, ever, let me go."

* * * * *

If you missed the previous story in the
Sons of a Parisian Dynasty trilogy,
then check out

Falling for Her Secret Billionaire

And if you enjoyed this story, check out
these other great reads from
Rebecca Winters

Capturing the CEO's Guarded Heart
Second Chance with His Princess
Falling for the Baldasseri Prince

All available now!